Fortune's Mail

Fortune's Mail

Greg Wright

authorHOUSE®

AuthorHouse™
1663 Liberty Drive
Bloomington, IN 47403
www.authorhouse.com
Phone: 1-800-839-8640

Published by AuthorHouse   01/09/2013

ISBN: 978-1-4772-9514-4 (sc)
ISBN: 978-1-4772-9515-1 (e)

Library of Congress Control Number: 2012922602

Any people depicted in stock imagery provided by Thinkstock are models, and such images are being used for illustrative purposes only.
Certain stock imagery © Thinkstock.

This book is printed on acid-free paper.

Because of the dynamic nature of the Internet, any web addresses or links contained in this book may have changed since publication and may no longer be valid. The views expressed in this work are solely those of the author and do not necessarily reflect the views of the publisher, and the publisher hereby disclaims any responsibility for them.

Part I

Discovery

───────── •◦• ─────────

ARTHROW SHARPSTRAIT WALKED UP TO the front of the archaic post office in the small town in Central Florida with his unusual yet determined gait. It was more of a marching pace really, with a precise pattern of lifting his foot, carrying it forward, and then dropping it straight down as if it had marionette strings. Weakened hamstrings as a child forced him into this unusual stride, and as he grew into manhood, he never really adapted another.

Approaching the concrete handicapped ramp, he breezed easily up the incline while reaching for his ring of keys. Being the postmaster of such a small town allowed for a very small ring, so it was easy to keep them in his pocket rather than on a zip line off of his belt. Having had one in his earlier career, when large banks of PO Boxes were present in the entryway of the post office, had proven cumbersome, and he always felt like he was pulled to one side.

But over the years as technology advanced and the demands that were required of his outpost became fewer, services and systems were moved to other locations, and his little postal office was determined to be expendable. The writing was on the wall, and he could read it clearly. It was only a matter of time before they would fade away. That time dawned a few months ago; he received the final notice of closure. Despite the services it provided, the seventy-three-year-old building and the eight employees would drift away from this area of Florida.

For some in the community, mostly the extremely isolated, their service symbolized the reach of a powerful, intrusive government, and its retreat symbolized a brushing away of the federal tentacle. But for the majority of the community, it was going to be a loss and an inconvenience. The nearest post office was twenty-three miles away on less than ideal roads.

He saw the end coming some years before and had only one desire—that he could stay there long enough before it closed so that he could take retirement rather than reassignment. He made it with four months to spare. The other carriers all received new assignments. Some of the eldest ones took an early package, less lucrative than a full-term retirement, but at least they had the opportunity to work at another vocation if they liked.

For him, the closing of the branch was the closing of a career. Both he and the building would slip away into an obscure existence regulated only by the rise and fall of the sun. Perhaps they would sell the building, and it would begin another life, but the chances of that were slight, as nothing new had been built in this area for years. The downtown itself, actually just four corners of low, brick buildings, were half full most of the year. Occasionally in the vacant front windows, posters and pictures were on display as contest winners from school functions, but these were only up for a short period; the sun always baked the colors, and they faded rapidly throughout the days. Just like the posters, this town was fading. A population of 2,100 was steadily evaporating as the attrition of age dwindled the old, and the continual state of unemployment drained away the others, who migrated to new areas for jobs or to be closer to family.

Reaching the front door; its clean, white paint reflecting the early morning sun and making it ten degrees hotter than it normally would be, he squinted from the glare, put the key into the lock, and swung the door open. The entryway was still shadowy, and as was his habit, he reached for the light switch and turned on the light banks for the main concourse. Granted, it was small, forty feet by sixty feet, but the tall ceilings and old-style architecture with the long paneled windows made it seem . . . grander.

Walking through the small hall, he skirted past the heavy fabric railings that formed the line in front of the counter and pushed through a small, swinging door that led behind it. There were three stations dividing the counter equally. One was never used, its machinery obsolete and covered with plastic, like putting a parrot away for the night. The second station was modernized but used only during the Christmas holidays. Nothing was uncovered, yet. Storage boxes and parcels were stacked and organized around the machines, making it more of a temporary docking station for transitioning paper.

He walked over to the station that was regularly in use and activated it. Next, he continued his way through a steel door in the wall behind the counters, which led back toward the sorting and departure area. The area was completely open, a beehive of activity with carts full of letters being pushed one way and attendants at every desk shuffling through the procedures and codes that defined the bureaucratic core. From the ceiling hung large fans, though they were not being used due to the air-conditioning now cooling the building.

A security wall had been erected behind the counter to control access to the rear. Facing the thick security door leading to the back, he remembered . . . another key. No sooner had he passed through the door than he heard someone banging on the metal accordion doors at the dock—three sharp raps, followed quickly by three more.

"Hold on!" he yelled. "Hold on! I'll be there in a minute!" His steps grew faster, yet just as precise as he reached the loading dock, rapidly clicking on the lights as he passed by the switches.

After kicking the latch free, he pulled down the loose, sagging chain that slowly winched up the door into its ancient steel roll. When it was halfway up, about ten feet, he stopped and looked down at the two thin men dressed in a postal uniforms staring back at him.

"Waiting long?" Arthrow shot at them.

The front man, appearing slightly perplexed, looked at the taller, skinny man behind him. The taller, blond one in the back replied, "No—not really?"

"Then what was with all the banging?"

"Just letting you know we're here, dude," the front man replied, suddenly feeling comfortable with the situation. "Just making a little noise." The last comment caused them both to grin sheepishly—thin, yellowish teeth nestled in the thicket of three-day-old beards.

Arthrow despised these subcontractors. They failed to understand the standards required and did only the bare minimum of what was asked, always succeeding to fail on the first attempt.

"Okay, boss," the first man began. He turned his baseball hat around while completing a perfect landing after making a standing thirty-inch vertical leap from the concrete onto the edge of the dock. With a spring in his step, he aimlessly wandered toward the vacuous mailroom. "What do we take out today?"

After helping the tall, far less agile, second man struggle onto the dock, Arthrow turned and attempted to catch up to the loose bull now wandering in his mentally organized pasture.

"Today you need to take some desks and filing cabinets. We already cleaned them out, so they're ready to be shipped. Please start . . ." The sound of a bell from the front counter signaled the arrival of a patron. As per his occupation, he turned to duty first. "Umm," he continued, now distracted, "over there, and I'll be back soon."

At a forced pace, he shot through the security door and slipped behind the first station at the counter. He was surprised to see not one, but three people waiting with packages and registered mail.

As he proceeded to dispense his services, he could hear the crash of metal on mortar and the tinkle of falling bolts, accompanied by the screech of sliding iron on bare concrete. Bouncing around the high ceiling, the collisions in the back seemed to be those of earthmoving tractors and steel girders, not office furniture.

Arthrow smiled politely, excusing the noise as he addressed each customer. The first two customers were easily dispensed with. The third and last customer was eighty-three-year-old Abigal Wintour, who finally angled her walker up to the counter after an egregious amount of time had passed. She asked what all the racket in the back was about.

"Well, Abigal, they're moving out furniture that we don't need in anticipation of our closing next month."

"Oh, you're closing?" she said mournfully, as if hearing of someone's sudden death.

"Yes, ma'am."

"But why? Is the government closing all of the post offices?"

"No, ma'am, just this one."

"Oh, I see." She paused, suddenly aware of the dilemma. She leaned her thin, small frame forward, its shape barely discernible in the threadbare blue sundress. "But where will I mail my packages?"

"You have to go to Cypress Grove. They will take care of you there."

"Will you be there?"

"No, ma'am. I'm retiring when they close this building."

"Oh, that's good." She raised her steeply arched eyebrows, painted in a dark pencil, and her reddened eyes widened. "That's good, right?"

A sudden "Watch out, dude!" followed by a sharp crash interrupted them.

"At this moment," Arthrow answered, "yes, it is."

"Thanks, boss!" came a grateful reply from the back.

"Well I just need to send this package to my son in California." She hefted a dense package, about the size of a shoebox, onto the counter from her walker, its weight causing her fingers to quiver from the effort. "He lives in Anaheim."

"I see," Arthrow replied as he pushed the package onto the scale. He gave her the rates and options, and she seemed confused. After a frustrating few minutes, she chose the least expensive.

"And how will you pay for this?" he asked.

"Oh, I will pay in cash as I always do." With unsteady hands and thin, whitish fingers, she proceeded to fumble in her purse located in the center of the basket on her walker. "You know, I always make strawberry preserves when they're in season, and I always make sure I send some to my boy. He really looks forward to it." Finding her small, wicker wallet, she pushed the snap about with a little help from a bend in her shoulder.

"How much is it again?" she asked.

"Forty-two dollars and sixty-seven cents."

Turning her wallet over, a paper clip, some odd coins, and a thin roll of green construction paper tightly bound in a rubber band rolled out.

"Let's see," she began as she carefully counted out the change. Amazingly, the sixty-seven cents were there. "And now," she continued, "you said forty-two dollars?"

"Yes. Yes, I did," Arthrow said with a heavy sigh.

"I thought so. See? I still have it," she said as she winked awkwardly. Snapping the rubber band, she unrolled the green construction paper that was cut into the exact size of a twenty-dollar bill only with the number twenty printed on each corner in thick black ink and a crudely drawn portrait in the center. Counting out three sheets, she presented them to him in a neat line.

"Here's sixty. I could use the change in ones please."

Staring at the paper before him and then her wide, shallow, clueless eyes, he struggled with how he was going to present reality to the dear woman. From the back, he heard the sound of stressed, bending metal, followed by, "Wow, it looks like a tepee."

At that moment, the cavalry arrived.

Florence Dawkins flew through the front door. Looking fresh and ready in her uniform, she slid her lunchbox under the counter and tapped Arthrow on the back of the arm. "So sorry I'm late. You would not believe what I've been dealing with this morning."

Seeing the art project laid out in front of him, and hearing the chaos in the back, she quickly assumed that there was no sense going forward with the rest of the excuse.

"You deal with this," Arthrow pointed at the counter with his left hand, "and I will deal with that," he said, pointing to the back with his right hand.

"Yes, sir!" she said. She addressed the woman in front of her with a low, concerned voice.

"But my husband used to print these in the barn all the time . . ." was the last thing he heard before entering the dock area.

Pushing back the solid door leading to the rear dock area, he was slightly taken aback by what the two loaders had sculpted. They stood, slightly perplexed, staring at two desks reared up on two legs with the other two legs lifted into the air and locked together. It appeared as if two rutting mustangs were engaged in mortal combat over a mare. Lying prostrate between them was a four-drawer filing cabinet, its drawers facing down, as if it had ducked down to avoid being a victim in the conflict.

"How did you do that?" Arthrow asked.

"Oh," began the shorter, somewhat embarrassed leader, "we were trying to pick up the cabinet, and the weight shifted inside . . . And then it went like *bam*, so we just like let it go so it wouldn't fall on us."

"Yeah," chimed in the second, "like one of us could have gotten hurt or something, and that would really have been bad for you."

"Yeah," Finished the first one, having gained confidence. "Like really bad for you with us being hurt, and you having to do all the paperwork and stuff." Convinced they had sold it, they looked at each other and nodded in compliance.

"What about the desks?"

"Ummm . . . same excuse—different furniture."

"I see. Well, we can't have it like that. Let me help you get them apart so you can get them on the truck."

Arthrow sighed and went over to help them separate the desks. Since they were empty, they were light, and it was just the physics of unlocking their steel frames that seemed to be difficult. After they were apart and on the truck, Arthrow turned to the dark green filing cabinet on the floor.

"Watch it, man, that bitch is heavy," the second hauler warned.

"Shouldn't be," Arthrow said as he surveyed the rectangular box in front of him. "All of these extra cabinets should be empty." Reaching down to grasp the top, he felt the weight in his shoulders begin to pull him over, and he stopped to gain his footing.

"Wow, it is heavy," he said, a little confused. This branch rarely kept paper files. He shifted his feet out a little farther to get a better angle on the cabinet. "Help me with this, and we will get this unit righted and on the truck."

Obediently, the two loaders bent down and grabbed an upper corner, one on either side of the top, while Arthrow held the center.

"Okay . . . on three. Ready?" They both nodded.

"One . . . two . . . three." Arthrow gasped at the immovable weight.

Realizing that "on three" meant "on three," the other two lifted a half beat later. Steadily, the cabinet rose like an obelisk directed at the sun, until it landed squarely on its base with a thud.

"Well done," Arthrow stated. Glancing at the yellowed, typed labels firmly attached to the ID boxes, he grasped a handle and pulled on the center drawer. It didn't budge. Arthrow pulled out his ring of keys and quickly singled out the master.

"Now, let's see what's in here," he said as the short, burnished key slipped into the cylindrical lock at the top of the cabinet. With a quick twist, the cylinder slid out, releasing the locks on the four drawers with a subtle click.

Firmly, he gripped the handle, released the middle drawer lock with his thumb, and pulled it forward. It rolled out easily, and Arthrow gazed into its treads.

Stacked somewhat haphazardly were large bundles of letters and cards wrapped with rubber bands and sealed in one-gallon freezer bags. He lifted one of the half-dozen or so bags and carefully peered through the plastic. All of the mail had been posted over the last few weeks or so but had never been delivered. Instead, it had been sorted and sealed here. Replacing the package back in the drawer, he closed it and opened the others. Two drawers held similar contents, with one package also containing a garage door opener. Pushing the button through the package, he listened carefully, the silence letting him know that it had nothing to do with this building.

In the bottom drawer, he found something a little more disturbing—loose editions of *Soldier of Fortune* magazine along with informational circulars on survivalist technics, firearms procurement, and how to prepare for the coming anarchy. Just glancing through it, he decided that was all he needed to see and slid the drawer closed.

"Sir, when this particular unit is clear, we will then proceed to remove it and place it on the truck," announced the first loader, speaking authoritatively so as to appear in control of the situation.

"Yes . . . yes . . . I know," Arthrow said distantly. He opened the top drawer again and studied the addresses more carefully. Gaining no clues, he turned to the two haulers studying the remaining desks in front of them. "Go ahead and get the rest of the furniture on the truck. Just leave this here for now."

"No problem, boss!" the lead man said. Then he continued to show his compatriot how best to position the two desks before them, using hand gestures with his over-sized gloves swinging like open cattle gates.

Arthrow sullenly walked past the desks toward his office in the back. After flipping out his keys, he unlocked the door, passed through it, and slowly closed it behind him. Sliding behind his desk, he rolled the chair back slightly, leaned it back, closed his eyes, and rubbed his forehead. He had heard of cases like this—a rogue mailman hoarding bundles of mail in an attic, basement, or garage. He never thought something like this could happen on his watch. He needed to think.

Who could it be?

In some ways, he was lucky. The size of their distribution area was convenient when the flow in the other branches was heavy. When the main center in

Scanlon was getting overwhelmed, it wasn't unusual to get a semi-sized courier here to be sorted and then shipped. Mail from all over the country would come here and then be re-distributed to where it needed to go.

The postmarks on the letters were dated around Mother's Day. It was a big shipping day, not as much as in the past, but big enough that a large carrier came in, and he brought two . . . no, three people in to sort. He thought about who had access to the mail when the obvious suddenly came to him. The key. It was a locked cabinet; only one other person had that key.

Leaning forward, he gazed about him at the thinning piles of paper, the folders slowly diminishing as the workload lessened and the end became more certain. At least the pictures of his family were easier to see.

Reaching over to the phone, he slid out a small, plastic index tray from underneath it and coasted his finger down the numbers until he reached the one he was looking for. After punching in the number, he cradled the phone between his shoulder and jaw as he leaned over his desk, forearms crossed, brow furrowed in contemplation of what he was going to say.

Three times the phone purred, and then a click, and a familiar voice came on the line.

"Livingston."

"Dave, it's Arthrow." There was a calm murmur. "No it's not that at all. The guys showed up, and they are loading everything up as we speak. Actually, I'm calling about something I found . . ."

Fortune's End

————————— •◦• —————————

EVEN THOUGH THE ALARM WAS set every night, Winthrop Fortune always rose before the hardened sound of the alarm shattered the morning air. It was set abrasively loud, designed for function. It was a habit that overruled an action, not the groundless paranoia of it waking him up in the early daylight suddenly unawares as to what time it was or where he should be. Every night at 9:49, he set his alarm for 6:15 the next morning. The intention was to be officially asleep by 10:00, giving him approximately eight hours of sleep with only a smattering of minutes over that designated time. Perhaps it was knowing that there was a backup plan in place that actually helped him sleep. Regardless, waking between 6:00 and 6:15 every morning, he turned the button on the clock/radio to off before it ignited a whole series of uncontrollable events and walked into the bathroom for his shower.

He clicked on the shower radio, set to an information station. Hanging by the fishing line (doesn't degrade as quickly at rope) from a small hook positioned in the tile wall, the radio hung just above the shower curtain such that the sound would fill the entire bathroom, and he could hear it clearly. Positioned lower, the sound became distorted in the narrow vacuum of the shower stall.

"News Radio 770 AM, the current time is now 6:08 a.m. with headlines every quarter hour and weather on the nines." An advertisement followed, changing the rhythm and tempo. Perfect timing. He had thirty seconds before the weather. *We'll see if any changes occurred overnight.*

Finishing his shower before 6:32 a.m. (including shaving), he then put on his white terrycloth robe, walked back into the bedroom, and began to set out his uniform for the day. Having worked for the United States post office for twenty-eight years, the colors were decided, with only the style combination dependent upon the weather conditions. He always made a point to watch the news channel at night just to make sure he knew what to expect the next morning. The radio then let him know whether to adjust it slightly one way or another.

Next, he strolled into the large walk-in closet at the end of the bedroom. Wool socks versus cotton, or perhaps on cooler days, one worn over the other. Fleece jacket versus Gore-Tex, depending on the chill. Bahamian helmet or baseball cap, depending on the heat. Having lived in southwest Florida most of his life, it was never the time of the year that was defining, but rather the time of the season. There were two, wet-hot and dry-cool, and with the daily record-low and the record-high separated by only four degrees.

Being October, the hot-wet season was slipping into the cooler, less humid, dry season. No more afternoon rains to be concerned about each day. Less rain gear, more sunscreen. He could feel the gradual slide in the temperatures throughout the weeks as the gulf winds shifted and the water temperature cooled.

He had organized his closet with his casual, or civilian, clothes on one side, and his uniforms (with shoes and coats) on the other side. Before, when he was married, he was forced to share. She had the left side, and his was on the right with his shirts and pants properly categorized by work/casual, dry/wet season, and with additional subcategories based on color, size, and sleeve length. He also positioned his shoes, belts, and ties accordingly, creating a compartmentalized, distinct, and functional wardrobe. Hers was always a mix of . . . something. Shoes cluttered below, pants hung apart widely with dresses intermixed with shirts and business suits. Every time she would ask for his help finding something, he would cringe and stomp his way into the closet. He always found it—she never did—and as his reward, she was forced to listen to another lecture on being organized and prepared.

But she never listened. At first she just smiled and promised to do better. But after a few months, she became less appreciative of his help, and he could remember the tension building in the silence. Finally, she stopped asking, which appeased him but created tardy issues, because she couldn't find what she wanted to wear, and money issues, because rather than spending time finding an item, sometimes it was easier to just purchase two or three more.

When Abigail hung up his shirts, she would mix in his professional white dress shirts with his white Arrow evening shirts. It was exasperating moving each shirt back to its correct position, open collar facing left, and then double checking the entire line to be sure nothing was missed. She would never space them correctly either—two and a half inches between shirts, three inches between slacks to maintain their lines. He would frown and remind her as he rearranged them, spacing them appropriately and in the proper places, knowing that the more they were moved, the greater the invitation for wrinkles.

He hesitated over his shirts as he thought back, and then he shuttered slightly as if chilled. Never again would he live like an animal for a woman. It was the longest seven months of his life.

Since she left, things had returned to the way they were through more definition and orderliness. He could still detect the faint stench of perfume from her business suits when he opened the closet door and the still air was turned. He had accepted that as a symbol, or reminder, of a terrible lapse in judgment. Now he had plenty of room, not only for the current array of twenty-first-century uniforms, but also those he had purchased and unfortunately outgrown in the past, which he posted at the end of the hanger post. Despite the 13.4 miles a day he walked, age was beginning to redefine his profile, and he had no choice but to adjust to the landscape as it re-contoured.

Selecting long pants and a short-sleeved shirt with a windbreaker, he laid them out on the bed as he proceeded to the kitchen for breakfast. The coffee that had already been set to brew the night before was waiting for him in the pot by the sink, and after he had poured a cup, he cut a quarter-inch slice of bread off of a loaf he had baked the night before and put it in the toaster. As the thin wires of the toaster warmed to an orange hue, he reached over to turn on the small TV he kept on the counter to his left.

Withdrawing his hand quickly as if burned, he hesitated. With all senses tuned in, he stared at the television, its silent gray screen and knobs waiting patiently for direction, the directive to begin the day with the morning news and weather. With the temperament of a sentinel, it stood ready.

The television usually faced him as he stood by the sink so that it was easy to use the faucet, empty a cup, or grab a quick snack. It was always at a thirty-degree angle in relation to the sink. Now it appeared to be slightly askew by an additional ten degrees. He had the odd feeling that someone had been in this room and had left a shallow presence.

Looking around slowly, he noticed that the faucet spigot was turned all the way to the right, just as he had left it the night before. His knives were in their block, all accounted for. The three decorated food tins of proportionately decreasing size, arranged along the backsplash, were still neatly aligned and orderly. The soap dish was properly aligned with the handles of the sink, positioned three inches from the cold-water handle.

Slowly turning and looking around the kitchen, he noted the locations of each appliance, cabinet, door, towel, and cup. Everything was as it should be. Taking a deep breath and letting it out slowly, he felt the intensity leave his brow, and his diligence relaxed. Perhaps he had moved the television errantly. There hadn't been anyone other than him in the kitchen for—well, it had been so long he couldn't remember.

With a snap, the toast emerged, startling him slightly. He was edgy now. Perhaps it had to do with the semi-annual reviews coming up this month, although he never scored less than 90 percent in the twenty-eight years as a postal official. Trying to dispel the paranoia, he shook his head sharply and reached for a plate in the cabinet above the toaster.

Positioning the slices of toast equally on the plate, he took a knife out of the silverware drawer directly underneath the counter and carried it and the plate over to the counter by the refrigerator. Facing the refrigerator, he opened it and blindly reached to the top shelf of the door. Touching the lid of the jar, he popped the grape jelly out of its slot. Approaching the toast, he unscrewed the lid and peered into the jar.

Yesterday, he thought he had enough to spread fully over two slices, but now he realized he might be just shy. Setting the lid and jar down next to the plate, he walked across the kitchen to the small pantry at the back of the house. A small window faced the diminutive backyard. In the early morning, a squirrel was slowly making its way across the fenced-in yard, sniffing carefully for any fallen nuts or seeds.

Opening the white louvered doors, a brilliant array of colors from the multitudes of canned goods, vacuum-sealed fruits and juices, cases of bottled water, and cartons of crackers and dried fruit greeted him. The array of spices and aromas created a uniquely sweet odor that gave him a sense of calm. Here was his survival pack, enough substance and foodstuffs to sustain him in a time of upheaval. He would never have to leave the house, secure with months of nourishment while the rest of the outside world fought for what was left like animals. Concerning the question of survival, he was determined to be the fittest.

Suddenly, his mouth went dry, his fingers tightened around the door handles in a death grip, and the hair on his forearm began to rise. The forty-eight-ounce peanut butter jar, the one located between the carton of jelly and the boxes of rice, was askew. It was turned slightly, such that the label wasn't aligned with the shelf. It was turned so that the top of the J was slightly out of view, like a ship approaching the end of the horizon.

Checking his peripheral vision, he noticed the squirrel suddenly raise its head and tail, on full alert, and then dash for the wooden fence in the corner, panicked. Before the rodent had even reached the wood, he was out of the pantry, slamming the doors as he sprinted away.

When he reached the living room, he heard the glass patio door behind him explode and the sudden rustle of bodies passing through it, followed seconds later by the deafening crush of splintered wood and the front door succumbing to the head of a 250-pound ram. Leaving the family room, his heart racing out of his chest with fear, his breath coming in short gasps, he heard the thud of footsteps approaching and a muffled cry of "Freeze!"

Reaching the bedroom, he threw himself on the bed, rolling over the edge so as to land in a crouched position between the bed and his dresser. Reaching toward his winter drawer, which slid underneath his bed, he yanked on it hard, such that it flew off its tracks, scattering grey and blue sweaters and insulated wool socks all over the floor. A glance told him it wasn't there, which was just as well, because by his left ear, he heard the hammer draw back on a revolver and a deep, stern voice whisper, "Don't move."

Obeying, he stopped moving as he heard three more loud clicks from three more hammers being pulled back. Having seen enough television, he slowly raised arms while rising to his feet. Turning around slowly, he saw the full extent of the invasion. Four SWAT officers were holding guns at his head from across the bed. Three of the weapons were Glock semiautomatic pistols while the third was an M-1A assault rifle. All of the officers were complete with assault gear, helmets, protective vests, and heavily tined face guards to lessen their chance of being identified.

The last man in his vision was the man who was directly behind him. Turning around, he saw a diminutive detective staring up at him through wire-rimmed glasses, his pale blue eyes glaring at him authoritatively over a thin, black mustache. The name Rosetti blazed across the upper right corner of his shield. The official was a full eight inches shorter than him.

"Looking for this?" he asked in a deceptively deep voice as he pulled out a rolled up, clear plastic bag from behind his obscenely oversized breast plate. With a snap, he unrolled it and displayed the remote box, just small enough to fit inside a man's pocket, and a .38 caliber handgun.

Realizing he was out of options, Winthrop fidgeted nervously. "You need a warrant to do this!" he protested. "It's against my rights to be treated like a psychopath."

The detective smiled. "Interesting choice of words," he said, and then from the other side of his breast plate, he produced what appeared to be a tri-folded brochure.

"While you're reading this, we'll take a look around." Turing toward the armed guards, he said, "Emerson, show Mister Fortune the sofa." Two detectives with pistols moved to walk him out of the room.

The guard with the assault rifle relaxed his stance, but not his aim, as he motioned for Winthrop to leave the bedroom and head toward the living room. After snatching the warrant from the small detective in a fit of frustration, Winthrop held it tightly in his fist as he was marched away, the two escorting officers a comfortable distance behind.

In the living room, another guard stood by the french doors. The room was beginning to swell with the radiance of the morning light pouring through the exceptionally clear glass of the doors. In the living room were all the usual accoutrements—sofa, bookshelf, a small drawing table with a computer, a recliner positioned squarely facing the TV. Taking a seat on the edge of his leather reclining chair, he sat at an awkward angle with his back straight. As he nervously flipped the warrant over and over, perspiration began to bead on his forehead and upper lip. The guard stood silently by his side, his rifle now at ease.

"This can't take long; I have to get to work," he said, his tone loud and edgy. Defiance had bled into excuse. Very quickly it tumbled into a request for mercy.

"I haven't done anything wrong," he began, looking at no one in particular. "I'm a simple man, just going to work and doing my job the best I can."

Turning to his guard, he tried the direct approach. "Do you realize I haven't missed a day or been late to work in eighteen years?"

"Until today," the policemen said.

Having lost his last appeal, the postman returned to his nervous twitching, staring at the blank television screen in front of him, which reflected his sullen image.

Walking into the kitchen, the detective was greeted by another detective casually drinking coffee despite the activity around him.

"So that's what we're looking for?" the young man asked Rosetti as the small, senior detective struggled to get out from behind his burgeoning tortoise-shell shield. The young detective watched patiently as his superior struggled with the clips on the side of the harness. He slowly took another sip of his coffee.

"Want help with that?" the young detective finally asked, sliding his idle left hand into his pants pocket, while he rotated the now empty coffee cup with his right.

"No thank you, Detective Murphy. I've been on many raids such as this, and taking these . . . uh . . .

vests off is second nature . . . uh . . . to me." His voice was muffled as the vest had now consumed his head, appearing much like a young carp in the mouth of a giant clam.

Nodding to two policemen standing nearby, Murphy stood by quietly as they shouldered their weapons, grabbed either side of the vest, and slipped it off of Rosetti, revealing a red-faced, sweaty, little man with round glasses, his awkward comb-over standing straight up in the air like an agitated cockatoo.

Sensing the dishevelment or perhaps a breeze across his bare pate, Rosetti reached up and slid his fingers through his hair, returning it to some semblance of a hairline. Sensing his embarrassment, Murphy reached over and flipped Rosetti's collar down in an attempt to help him get his appearance organized.

"To answer your question, Detective," Rosetti began, "yes, this is what we came here for."

He cracked the seal on the Ziploc bag with a loud snap and reached in.

Standing in the kitchen, Murphy and the two guards watched as Rosetti pulled out a small, gray, circular remote with a single white button in the center. Lifting their visors to see better, one of the policemen scratched his small, black moustache while the other just gave his a quick swipe to get the moisture out.

"Looks like the remote to a garage door," Murphy said, a little disgusted and mentally trying to figure out a way to get his name off of this report, as this was now on the fast track to being a fiasco.

"It is," Rosetti began, "but not to a garage door." He pressed down on the button.

They stared blankly at each other as the sudden rumbling of chains on steel filled the kitchen . . . it's origin from behind the closed door leading into the garage from the kitchen. Taking a deep breath, Murphy closed his eyes, crumbled up the Styrofoam cup, and tossed it into the sink. He reached for the radio on his hip. The other two officers, stunned slightly by the awkwardness of the situation, glanced at each other, at the remote in Rosetti's hand, and then again at each other.

"Officer Schell."

"Yes, Detective," responded a voice over the speaker.

"Please make sure you inventory and search everything in the garage."

"Yes, sir," the voice answered.

Murphy shook his head as Rosetti stared darkly at the remote, hurt and angered by its betrayal.

"Ah . . . Detective?" the voice suddenly crackled back.

"Yes, Schell?" Murphy answered as he began walking out of the kitchen toward the front door where Schell and a second team of investigators were waiting in the driveway.

"Since you're inside, could you please open the garage door for us?"

Murphy stopped. Rosetti suddenly looked up, a meek smile of vindication beginning to brighten his rounded face. The two policemen, still confused, shifted uncomfortably as they awaited orders.

"The garage door is open," Murphy answered. "I heard it from the kitchen."

There was a long silence, during which Murphy bolted toward the front windows that looked out onto the driveway.

"Sir . . . uh." It was obvious Schell was tactfully trying to sculpt a reply. The officer clearly remembered being on the front of a door ram as they pounded through a suburban split-level home, hoping to find a meth-amphetamine lab and instead discovering the Daughters of the Confederacy experimenting with their own recipe for raspberry tea. To this day, even the smell of a mixed berry ChapStick makes him wince.

"Could we have a verification of address . . . sir, please." His tone thick with the threat of embarrassment, but Murphy was already at the window, watching Schell and the three other young officers standing in the driveway, a hand on each of their gun belts and another holding a thick clipboard.

"Stand by, Schell." Murphy said. He turned to go back into the kitchen to the door leading to the garage, but he was blocked by Rosetti, armed with fresh confidence and two curious policemen.

Pushing through the door, the garage was dark and musty. The smell of gas and lawn chemicals mixed with stale air. The garage door was definitely closed, but above it, in the center of the ceiling, one end of a well disguised stairway had lowered on a mechanized lift, allowing entrance into the loft above. By the side of the kitchen, a red light showed the location of the opener for the garage door, and with authority, Rosetti hit it with his fist. As the garage door opened, Rosetti smiled broadly and rubbed his newly bruised hand.

As daylight slowly illuminated the room, the elaborate engineering of the remote-controlled stairway became apparent. It was a thin stairway, barely wide enough for a man, with one end lowered by chains from a small opening in the ceiling, which was loosely covered with drywall on the outside to match the color of the garage. It was perfectly disguised and secure.

Cautiously, Murphy strode over to the stairway. Rosetti had already raced to the stairs and had bounded up them. Once in the attic, the sound of three solid footsteps was then greeted by silence. Looking up into the hole, Murphy and the two officers were joined by Schell and his three attendants, anticipating the grim finding of an ex-wife or rolls of extra insulation.

They listened as the heavy sound of rustling plastic and the thud of heavy objects moved toward the stairs. Suddenly, a black garbage bag flew down the stairs and landed in the middle of them. It was followed very quickly by two others, their yellow drawstrings neatly folded into bows.

A fourth followed, and the edge of the bag caught on one of the metal clips that held the springs to the dropdown door. Suddenly, armloads of bundled letters tumbled out into the air. They covered the existing bags and fell over the officers staring in the wonderment at parcels from the sky.

Four letters landed directly in Murphy's hands as he grabbed at them, mostly in self-defense. The other officers picked up letters and tried to digest what they were seeing.

"This has a twelve-cent stamp," said one policeman.

"That's because it's from 1975," Murphy said.

"Here's '86, '92, '78 . . ."

"Mine are all from '89."

"That's just the few bags I saw near the stairs!" Rosetti yelled down from the crawlspace. "All the eaves up here are full."

Murphy looked up, somewhat shocked at the intensity of Rosetti's red-faced, boyish grin as he leaned over the entrance to the apparent archive.

Picking up a couple of additional letters, Murphy studied the lettering and script as he walked back into the house. One of the letters was written in styled longhand, likely written by a woman, and its stiffness gave away its contents as a card of some sort. Another was in a halting, brittle script, possibly written by an elderly man. Another was typed. The senders and recipients were from all over the country, and all had been stamped, tagged, and processed through the system. None were unopened.

Walking through the kitchen and into the living room, he approached Winthrop, the letters flayed before him like a hand of cards. Winthrop was sitting rigidly, his eyes staring straight ahead, his hands folded serenely in between his knees, as the detective confronted him.

"These go back almost twenty years," Murphy said, as he folded the letters together into a tight packet as if closing on a hand of cards. "Why did you keep these?"

Silence.

A bead of sweat appeared by Winthrop's ear, rolled to his jaw, and followed the jaw line to his chin.

"These are all letters from mothers to their sons, from brothers to brothers, and grandparents to grandkids." Murphy stopped, seeing his inquisition wasn't getting him any information.

"A waste," Winthrop suddenly blurted out. "They were wasting their time and mine. Why should I submit to their whims when if they really cared for each other, they would just visit each other or call on the phone?" Suddenly stopping, he pushed the bead of sweat away from his chin with the knuckle of his thumb.

"You realize this is a serious felony. You are looking at some long, hard time here."

For the first time, Winthrop looked at him. His eyes were dark and seemed to have sunken in. "In another age, I would have been a kingmaker, a trusted advisor. Someone who could glean away all the detritus of chatter and present only true matters of importance, those correspondences that were of true consequence and not this collection of . . . of," he waved an open hand as if dismissing a nuisance, " . . . of . . . useless drivel. It all has a shadow of death to it. Of endings." He then resumed his catatonic stare, wiggling his finger in a twitch of nervous energy.

Pursing his lips, Murphy tapped the envelopes on his thigh. As a police officer, nothing Winthrop had just said seemed pertinent. Perhaps to a psychiatrist it would. Leaving him to his guards, Murphy shoved his open hand in his pocket and strode back through the house. Stepping over the splintered doors and damaged walls, he noticed the house was now an official crime scene with technicians taking evidence, tape marking boundaries, and plastic bags filled with papers, artifacts, and small books began to fill larger, brown evidence boxes.

Walking back into the garage, Murphy caught sight of the flashes through the opening in the ceiling. A camera in the attic was photographing the bags of evidence exactly as they were found.

"Detective?" an officer said from over Murphy's shoulder.

Turning, he saw a young officer standing next to a stout, elderly female postal worker with a crew cut and badly sun-damaged cheeks.

"The lady here," he shifted uneasily at the description, "would like to know if she can take the bags."

Murphy thought for second. "I think we only need a small percentage as real evidence." After pausing to recall his regulations, he spoke more assuredly. "Yes, she can take the bulk of it, but," he smiled slightly as he glanced at the U.S.P.S. jeep parked just off the driveway apron, "you're going to need a bigger truck."

"You realize that this is another poor reflection on the US postal service," the mailwoman suddenly blurted out with the directness of a drill sergeant screaming at a recruit under the barbed wire. "We just got past the 'going postal' jokes—and now this."

Murphy nodded in acknowledgment as he walked out to a parked squad car in the driveway. Reaching into the backseat through the open window, he pulled out a glazed donut.

"Kind of like cops and donuts!" He yelled back. Biting into it, he turned and walked away. "Get past it," he mumbled just loud enough for her to hear as he walked back to his own car.

Part II

Evelyn's Letter

THE REGULATION BLUE AND WHITE mail truck pulled alongside the grey mailbox on the dirt county road as it had for so many years. A worn tire path stretched from the edge of the road, creating a shallow crescent, its apex being the mailbox with the rusty hinges and once-red metal flag, now leached to a subtle pink by the endless summers of brilliant Iowa sun. Being late summer, the weeds between the path and the road had established a thin colony of pioneer chicory, remarkably shorter than its ancestors due to the daily pressure and heat of a jeep muffler, yet resilient in its attempts to flower, seed, and perpetuate the species.

The driver reduced speed to a slow crawl while he double-checked the sort. Without looking up, he instinctively hit the brake as the open passenger side aligned with the mailbox. The abrupt stop caused a ten-foot tall metal whip fastened to the back bumper, which held a slow-traffic diamond, to slap against the top of the cab with the sharp crack of snapped metal. For a few seconds, the rod quivered before standing sentry still.

In the farmhouse, Evelyn Moorehouse walked toward the front door. After wiping pie dough off her hands with a kitchen towel, she opened the screen door and stood on the long, open porch that wrapped around half the house like a moat. The sound of the whip against the cab meant a stopped truck, and that usually meant a package that couldn't be readily placed in the box. As she began to walk down the stairs, the truck suddenly jolted forward, pausing briefly for a quick wave from the postman, and then quickly reached speed as it proceeded toward the next farmhouse. She waved back, not with a shy flip of the wrist, but with a fully stretched arm and a spinning hand. Her mother had always said to be polite and gracious, particularly being a woman, because the opportunity to meet people was so rare this far away from town. Enthusiasm was not only appreciated, but required.

Reaching the black asphalt driveway, she felt the warmth from the tar percolating through the thin, worn rubber of her deck shoes. They had the driveway blacktopped last year when she inherited the house after her mother died. Being the only child, she received everything—the house and buildings, 1,200 acres, with a small mill pond next to a small copse of wood where she played as a child with her cousins.

She and her husband of fifteen years, Dale, had been farming the land ever since they had been married, and with the combined acreage that he had already owned and rented, it added up to almost 8,000 acres of prime farmland. Her mother's passing presented a validation of sorts rather than an inheritance.

Walking down the same driveway she had walked her whole forty-two years, she reached the mailbox, skirting the nests of ground wasps circling in the gravel by the road along the way. She regarded the regulation postal hinge. Being a heavy metal, the latch was very hot on this summer day, so using her apron as a buffer, she opened the lid quickly.

Skimming through the half-dozen or so envelopes, she nodded at the usual correspondence before tucking the bundle under her arm and reaching down for a large, thick envelope leaning against the base of the weathered, white wooden post.

At first, the brilliant white of the paper blinded her, and she blinked slightly as she read the return address. It was a somewhat heavy package, and the return address was from the postmaster general of Ft. Myers, Florida. She bounced it into her right hand as she retrieved the bundles from under her arm with her left. Grouping them all together, she closed the mailbox door, lowered the flag, and began the walk back up to the house.

Entering the living room, she glanced at the heavy wooden wall clock and began planning the afternoon logistics for lunch. Her husband and the two boys were working the fields nearby, so they would be in for lunch. Leftover meatloaf and mashed potatoes would suffice, yet for some reason, she couldn't turn toward the kitchen. Her feet now seemed planted, and the package kept drawing her attention. Finally deciding to temper her curiosity, she placed the regular mail on the table next to the sofa and dropped into the recliner. Placing the package squarely on her lap, she stared at the labels, wondering if somewhere in the addresses and numbers there was a clue. But it only revealed the simplicity and mendacity of a never-ending service bureaucracy.

As she slid her finger under the flap, it resisted her efforts at first—resolute in its barrier of tamper-proof packaging—yet it was no match for her strong fingers, toughened by years of outdoor work, indoor meals, and three years of semi-pro softball. With the flap quickly reduced to a ragged edge, she reached in and pulled out dozens of letters and cards all addressed to her mother. In astonishment, she shuffled through them, their aged paper crackling at the touch, postmarks barely discernible, and handwritten addresses slowly fading away from time. There were postmarks from 1975 and 1982, but none from later than 1995.

In amazement, she saw postcards from her grandparents' Hawaiian anniversary trip in 1984, birthday cards from relatives long deceased, and Christmas cards from friends long forgotten. In the middle of the pile were utility and department store bills from companies that had been bought and sold and whose names could only be found in ancient financial history.

Noticing a few smaller letters, she reached into the envelope to retrieve the final bundle. She instead pulled out a clean white postcard neatly typed with an authentic signature. "Dear Postal Customer," it began.

Through a fortunate discovery by our investigative branch, we were able to locate many parcels of mail previously determined to have been lost. As required by law and our obligation to you, we are completing the service you have entrusted us with. Our sincerest apologies for any inconvenience this may have caused you.

Sincerely,
Trent Douglas
Attorney General
Ft. Myers, FL

"Huh," she said and slipped the paper back into the envelope. Feeling a crackle of paper on her fingernails, she retrieved one small envelope, relatively thin, that hadn't come out with the others. Finding its edge, she removed it while setting the empty package down next to the recliner.

All the return address said was Baxter, and it was addressed to her from Manatee Park, Florida. Seeing the name, her fingers suddenly began to tremble, and her heart set a racehorse's pace. Slowly becoming blinded by the tears, she dropped the letter and buried her face in her hands to absorb the sobs.

Speeding up the driveway, Dale honked his horn, announcing of his arrival. Pulling beside the house onto a gravel apron off the paved driveway, he hit the horn one more long time as his oldest son, a nineteen-year-old with blue eyes and sun-bleached hair, opened the passenger door and sprinted toward the front porch while Dale's younger son of sixteen jumped out of the back bed and followed his brother in hot pursuit. Laughing, the oldest allowed the second one to get just close enough, and then followed with an elbow to the chest just as he was pushing through the door. Caught off guard momentarily, the youngest quickly regained his balance and was able to push his brother through the door. While the boys fought their way into the house, Richard reached for his empty coffee cup from this morning and opened the truck door, sliding his keys into his jean pocket as he did. Immediately he knew something was wrong. While there was usually music coming from the open kitchen window, located right under the parked truck, as his wife prepared lunch, it was silent. He didn't hear her yelling at the boys to calm down, or the sounds of cracking plates and the tingle of bunched silverware. He was getting uncomfortable as he jogged to the front porch. Quickening his pace as he approached the steps, he heard his oldest son say, "Mom, are you okay?"

Vaulting through the open door, Dale saw the two boys standing at the entrance to the living room, completely still. Dale slid between them and placed himself between his sons and his distressed wife. She was still in the recliner, slumped like dead weight into the thick leather, her left hand shielding her eyes while her right hand clutched a small tumbler of clear liquid. No ice. She was breathing softly, pulsed by an occasional soft sob, but otherwise very still.

He took in the scene quickly and worked to manage his sons. "Your mom's okay, boys." Surveying the room quickly, he saw the opened letter on the floor, the remaining mail placed neatly by the chair, the opened box of tissue on its side next to it, and the opened bar in the corner of the room with the new liter of Bombay gin opened and missing almost a quarter of its contents. The red cap seal lay torn and crumpled on the bar like a dead snake on a hot road.

Turning to them, he forced a smile. "Go on upstairs, boys, and get cleaned up for lunch." They had never gone upstairs to clean up before—there was a bathroom right next to the kitchen—but they understood they were to be upstairs until summoned. Hesitantly they obeyed, charging up the stairs with far less enthusiasm than when they entered the house.

When he was confident they were out of earshot, he walked over to the chair and kneeled down in front of her, but her grip tightened, and she pulled the glass back toward her. He looked into her eyes, still shielded by her hand, and saw the steely blue stars of a woman deeply hurt and suddenly vulnerable, yet building a courage fueled by rage. He swallowed hard; he might be entering the bear's den.

"Who died?" he asked softly, fishing.

"Read the letter," she said icily, a tear streaming down her cheek like a drip from a leaky faucet. "Read the damn letter." Slowly, she brought the glass to her lips and took a long drink as Richard delicately reached for the paper on the floor. Holding it carefully by the edges, he stood up, walked over to the sofa, and sat down on the edge of the cushion.

"Dearest Evelyn," it began.

August 15, 1981

By now you know that I have left. It was a difficult decision, but one that I had to make in order for all of us to survive. It has been almost a month, and I have missed all of you terribly, but feel in my heart that this was for the best. I think of you and your mother constantly, but the happiness you will find in your future will surpass the pain you have felt or are feeling now.

It is difficult for me to express the reasons why I had to leave, they are very difficult for even me to understand, but I want to assure you that they do not involve you. All I have is love and amazement at the things you do, and missing you grow up fills me with a regret that I will carry with me throughout my life. Do the best you can in this life, and I hope you find the happiness I was unable to attain. When you are old enough, I hope you come to see me. Perhaps then we can build something new. All my love.

Dad

Dale folded the letter carefully on its seams and set it down next to the unopened letters. It had brought everything back. Dale remembered when he disappeared. There were few secrets in a small farm town, particularly when the manager of the grain elevator fails to report for work and is never seen again. He also remembered what had happened to the family a few months before. Evelyn had a brother about eight years younger than her. One afternoon, Evelyn's dad was using the tractor to haul some hay wagons when he stopped at the house to run in and pick up his gloves. He had turned the engine off and put on the brake before jumping off and dashing into house. The brake, which he had just fixed the day before, came loose, and the entire unit began to roll down the driveway toward the small boy playing by the ditch at the end of the driveway.

When he came out of the house, the tractor and wagons had rolled into the ditch, and the boy was face down in the center of the driveway, black checkmarks tattooed over his yellow collared shirt. The police guessed that he saw the runaway rig and tried to jump on it to stop it, only to slip and fall beneath the tires. It had killed him instantly.

"I was at basketball practice, and Mom was late picking me up," she said. "Only . . . Mom didn't pick me up. It was my Uncle Fred and Aunt Edith. Edith held my hand in the backseat as she told me, and we both cried until we got to the hospital."

Evelyn stopped and took a long swallow of gin. "Mom and Dad were there, but it was over. Nothing anybody could do." Her voice was becoming fainter, as if the trip into the past was slowly pulling her back with it.

Dale remembered the funeral. The whole town came out. The boy was buried in the family plot behind their house, and later when her Mom died, Evelyn placed her next to him.

Her father, Andrew, took a week or two off and then went back to the grain elevator, but his work was poor, riddled with errors made by a lack of concentration. His attendance was spotty for about a month, and then he was gone.

Dale sat for a few minutes more and then walked over to her. Bending over, he kissed her forehead. The cool skin against his lips reminded him of how close she was too him and how blended they were. As an affirmation, he could feel her forehead lean toward him, accepting the intimacy. Softly, he walked to the entrance of the living room and reached his arms across its expanse, hooking his fingers into two metal tabs on the face of the door jams and pulling out the thick, wooden packet doors. With a soft rumble, they rolled until their locks met in the center, sealing Evelyn and her past off from the rest of the house.

Dale went to bed alone that night as Evelyn faced the past in the four corners of the living room. Recovering from the shock and numbed by the gin, she walked over to the antique drawing table and pulled out the thin, heavily varnished center drawer. Reaching in, she pulled out a 5x7 snapshot of her, her mother, father, and Andy, her little brother. She was standing in front of her parents and smiling, showing new braces and the framework of a growing woman, while her brother, Andy, sat on the thickly treaded tire that would be his undoing a few weeks later.

There were plenty of other photos, but they were carefully boxed away in the attic. She kept this one available because it was the last photograph taken of them together, and the likeness between the father and son was becoming uncanny. As if receiving his father's name also entitled him to the likeness thereof.

The tears once again welled in her eyes, and she blotted them to see clearly. The bottom of the photograph was faded and blurred where so many times the tears had fallen. The family dog, Snoopy, who had managed to slip into the photograph and was seated neatly in front of her, was slowly being turned into a white and brown cloud of himself.

When she took out the photograph to remind her of her brother, it was usually to see how close they were, how they laughed and tormented each other to the verge of tears. But now she wanted to see her father, and as if noticing him of the first time, she tried hard to see past the anger and disappointment.

She could only assume what the picture gave her, a clean-cut man wearing black trousers and a crease sharp enough to chop wood. A clean, white shirt slightly ruffled at the collar showed the recent absence of a tie, something he always wore to church and quickly removed after the service, which was when this photo was taken.

He was sharp, intelligent, quiet most times, but very direct when the occasion arose. A strident perfectionist when it came to standards for himself, he seemed to allow for exception in his children. To make mistakes was part of growing up, he used to say; just learn from it and don't do it again. Mother was the disciplinarian, father was the moralist.

As plain as he was in his dress, so were his personnel habits. Regular haircuts kept the hairline just above a stubble. As his hairline receded, Mother used to say his head looked like a worn baseball diamond, a lot of bare patches with a sparse infield of grass. He would smile, hide behind the newspaper, and never change a thing.

He never smoked or chewed tobacco for one reason only. "It's bad for you," he would answer to an offer of either. He presented it as an absolute, not a choice, although he thoroughly enjoyed the company of those who did. Never speaking openly of politics, he listened intently to those who had an opinion as if he was a megaphone they could talk into and expect to be heard. His only emotions were for his family, and they were powerful and resolute.

On his right hand, she saw the wedding ring he wore only on Sundays. He didn't wear it during the week because he had seen too many men lose fingers when the metal was caught on a gear or lever. It wasn't his finger he was afraid of losing, rather the ring. Hanging slightly out of his pants, she saw the gold chain that looped from his belt buckle to the watch deep in his pocket. She seldom saw it. He revealed it only when a school function was about to start or a preacher talked beyond the forty-five minutes he had patience for.

Setting the photograph on end, she placed it toward the back of the desk so it faced her. Suddenly defiant, she crossed her arms and stared back at the young man in the photograph. "So you wanted me to come see you?" she stated aloud, jutting her chin as an expletive. "Huh!" she exclaimed.

Dale remembered that Evelyn came to bed late, very late, and he felt her crawl next to him, the touch of her hands and legs still holding the coolness of the room while the warmth of her cheeks and nose rubbed softly against his shoulder. Without opening his eyes, he rolled his head, kissed her softly on the forehead, and drifted back off to sleep, her presence filling him with comfort.

When he woke up, she was already out of bed and out of the room. It was not unusual, so he rose, dressed, and headed toward the boys' rooms.

"Get up, boys," he bellowed. "We have to get the lower acreage done today before the rain sets in this afternoon."

He noticed the storage closet in the hallway was left ajar. It was a walk-in where they kept the suitcases. Curious, he gazed into the expanse and didn't notice anything missing—only some boxes of holiday decorations pushed to the side and the suitcases jumbled together. Closing it, he reaffirmed the strength of the lock before heading downstairs, reassured the boys were getting up by the sounds of stumbling and moaning coming from behind their closed doors.

Reaching the bottom of the stairs, he strode into the kitchen. It was spotless and clean with no disturbance except for the slow hiss of the coffee pot spitting out the last of a fresh brew. With the absence of Evelyn, there was the absence of breakfast. Noticing the coffeepot set on a time brew, he then focused on the letter next to it.

Dearest Dale,

I adore you beyond any feelings that I have ever had for anyone, and I am not leaving you. The letter from my father opened up many buried feelings, and they are overwhelming me. I wasn't prepared for this, and reliving the past has raised so many questions and so much anger that I cannot function as before. I am going to Florida to see what is there. Probably, there isn't anything, but making the effort may help me finally close some doors on my doubts. I have already booked a flight home in a few days, and I promise I will be on it. Don't worry about me, I will be okay, please take care of the boys. I love you so, and I will miss you every day I'm away.

Love always, Ev

P.S. I baked some cinnamon bread last night for your breakfast, and it is in the refrigerator. Please don't cook while I'm gone. Margie will have everything you need.

He read the letter twice, touching the water marks on the bottom of the page. Just then, the boys came stumbling in, hair askew, shirttails out, and eyes still puffy with sleep.

"Where's breakfast?" the older one asked, followed by a brief silence and then the asking of a larger question by the youngest.

"Where's Mom?

Gathering her small, white carry-on bag, she struggled to get out of her seat as the others on the plane angled for position in the aisle. Being by the window was nice for the trip, but at the final sound of the departure order, it was the true measure of survival of the fittest to get to the exit. As the passengers at the front thinned out, she was able to edge her way into the aisle, and with the help of the kind young man from Des Moines who sat next to her during the trip, she was able to quickly retrieve her suitcase out of the overhead compartment and follow in line with the others.

As she approached the cabin door, the thin, cool air began to thicken slightly, and she could smell the sweetness of succulent flowers. Reaching the door, she hesitated at the top of the stairs leading out of the plane and into the terminal. The humidity was thick and felt like paste in her lungs. Her skin tingled as her blood curdled to adjust to the sudden change from cool and dry to hot and wet. Trying to catch her breath, she felt the warm, firm hand of the stewardess on her elbow.

"Are you all ready, ma'am?" she said politely. Evelyn turned to face the small, blonde woman half her age and half her size.

"Is it always this hot here?"

The stewardess never broke her smile. "I'm afraid so, ma'am."

"It's like a jungle."

"Actually, it's a swamp." The stewardess cocked her head and dropped her eyelids in sympathy. "First time?" she asked.

Nodding, she headed down the metal stairs, her suitcase banging loudly at each step. By the time she reached the bottom, the perspiration had already pooled in her armpits.

Pushing a stream of sweat from the corner of her eyes, she progressed across the hot asphalt.

The comfort of her foamed tennis shoes now worked against her as she felt the warmth percolate through the rubber and the humidity thicken her white, cotton socks with sweat. Now, as if in a revelation, the fundamentals and function of the open-toe sandal became obvious.

The automatic doors of the terminal readily slid open to receive her, as if they were the open arms of sanctuary itself. Pausing briefly inside, she felt the other passengers shuffle past her toward friends at the gates and waiting cars in the parking lots. Regaining her strength and breath, she headed toward a nearby information booth. Somewhere in this small terminal there was a rental car with her name on it. Walking around looking for it was not an option.

There were two people behind the information counter. One, a young black man, was smiling eagerly, his thin frame almost shadowed by his oversized uniform. The badge on his neatly pressed shirt seemed to fall forward and onto the desk for lack of shoulders to hold it back. At that angle, the nametag with Emmitt, spelled out in gold letters on a black background, seemed to address only the desk in front of him.

Next to him was an older, round woman. Her black hair was streaked with grey and white, yet her black skin had a youthful sheen to it. She too had the uniform and badge and a nameplate that said Ruby. She had a stern, lean glare as Evelyn approached. She was unnerving, and Evelyn was glad Ruby was preoccupied with another woman, so that only Emmitt was available. Despite her distraction, Ruby seemed to be studying Evelyn very closely even as she was handing a brochure to a red-haired woman in brown Capri pants.

As Evelyn approached the desk, she dropped her bags and wearily placed her elbows on the counter. While Emmett leaned forward, Ruby seemed to lean back with a severe, studied look.

"How may I help you?" he asked with a slight Bahamian accent and a flash of bright, white teeth. Evelyn searched through a side pocket before bringing out some slips of paper with hurried numbers written on them. When she arose, Ruby had her back turned and was talking quietly to a custodian she had pulled aside.

Emmitt deciphered the numbers and began the flow of information that would present a white sedan with less than thirty thousand miles at her disposal.

"I need some form of identification, please," Emmitt requested. His concentration on the computer screen was unwavering as he cautiously typed in the needed information. Reaching down into her satchel, she pulled out her wallet and then removed her ID. Rising, she handed it forward, only to have it intercepted by Ruby, who had finished her conversation and reached out for the card with silver-ringed fingers and long, red nails. As a true gatekeeper, she studied the small plastic card.

"What is your reason for visiting?" Emmitt inquired. "We always ask in case there's other information you may need that we can help you with," he added apologetically.

Not quite sure how to answer the question, she began with a known answer—her real reason for visiting the city. "Well, you may not believe this," she started, still trying to organize the facts.

"You are here to look for your father," Ruby answered, smiling and showing a strong line of gold laced teeth.

Evelyn stood there stunned. She gazed at Ruby and could see the hard almond eyes that had studied her for so long begin to mellow and soften. Emmitt stopped what he was doing as if frozen. His eyes darted awkwardly from Evelyn to Ruby and back again.

Suddenly, rescued from pretense, Evelyn could only agree. "Yes," she said softly.

Ruby nodded knowingly.

"You're lucky. Your search has ended before it began." She shifted her gaze from Evelyn to a lone figure leaning over a banister on the second floor above them.

Her father stood there with his elbows flat on the wooden rail, one leg crossed over the other, just as she remembered him standing as he judged lambs during the spring. Next to him leaned a mop in a brilliant yellow, wheeled bucket. His uniform consisted of a dull gray shirt and pants. Although his hair was thinner and his shoulders lower, it was her father.

With a sharp nod toward the staircase to the right of him, he smiled and casually walked toward it, leaving the mop and bucket.

"I'll watch your bag, dear. Just leave it right there in the front of the counter," Ruby said.

Emmitt shuffled his shoulders, the folds of his over-sized shirt moving only slightly. Staring blankly, he could only smile like a zombie.

As requested, Evelyn left her bag by the counter and looked over to a bench where her father had walked down to and stopped by.

"My coat too?" she asked, suddenly realizing its bulky shape over her arm.

"Yes!" Emmitt said enthusiastically, having received the cue he needed for involvement. Taking her coat, he placed it behind the counter while she shifted her purse to her shoulder and walked toward the bench. Suddenly feeling weak in the knees, images of her childhood began to filter through her mind, and the emotions began to well up until he stood before her, his arms open, smiling. She felt the cool wetness of the tears streaming down her cheeks.

She walked into his arms with strength she didn't think she had and buried her nose into his shoulder as he swallowed her into his arms.

The starch of the shirt was strong, but as she breathed through it, she remembered his smell, the smell that was there when she was a little girl and was going outside in the winter. Grabbing the nearest scarf on the peg, she had grabbed his by mistake, and as she braved the elements, she felt warm and secure because he was warm and strong, and she could smell him holding her. It was a perfume that was solely his, and it filled the air in the morning as she kissed him, and it blended in with the sausage and bacon and eggs that filled the kitchen each day. It was the smell that greeted her as she was clearing out her mother's closet and saw his shirts still hanging there after all the years. She took a flannel shirt out, it's red and yellow checks faded with age, and she buried her face into it and breathed him in one more time, as if he too was there to say good-bye to her mother.

She felt the strength of his arms pulling her tight and the soft pat of his hand as he whispered, "I've missed you."

Pulling away, she inhaled deeply and gulped in a sob. "Do you know about Mom?"

"Yes, I do," he answered. "Actually, I was getting a hometown paper mailed to me until just a few years ago. Now I get everything online through the library." He smiled a broad smile, the gap in his teeth still showing, and the lines by his eyes deeper and longer. Despite the age, he was still there in all his posture, poise, and perception.

"Let's sit down," he said, motioning to the empty seat before them. There were only a few people left in the terminal now that the arrivals had begun to clear away, so despite the openness, their privacy was assured. Sitting down next to each other, her father suddenly saw the need and produced a clean, white handkerchief that he presented to her so she could wipe away her tears.

After they settled in, he smiled once more, crossed his legs, and looked directly into her eyes. "I hoped you would come one day. Although I'm surprised it took so long," he said, following the sentence with an awkward chuckle.

"Well, actually, you may not believe this, but I just now got the letters you sent."

His incredulous stare called for some sort of verification, so she reached into her purse and produced the yellow, recently folded letter and presented it to him. Without a word, he took it, unfolded it carefully, and gazed at the words he had written years before.

"At first I thought it was a hoax, but then I read it over and over and over, and then I thought, *If it is real, what the heck*. Would it hurt just to show up and maybe just look around?" She hesitated and then asked the question she suddenly realized needed to be asked. "But what are you doing here?"

He hesitated, still drawn by the envelope, and then began his answer. "Well, when I sent the letter, I started showing up here whenever there would be planes flying in from Chicago or Des Moines or St. Paul, thinking that you'd be on one of them someday. After a time, I started running out of money, and since I was here pretty much every day anyway, I applied for a job, and they hired me. After a time, I made friends with the stewards, and they let me scan the passenger manifests for your name." Realizing the letter was still in his hand, he passed it back to her as cautiously as he had received it. "When I saw your name on the list yesterday, I was overcome. Didn't sleep last night. I told Ruby to keep an eye out for you."

"That's how she knew who I was. I thought she was a witch or something."

He smiled. "She pretends she is, but I think it's so the boss doesn't fire her. He's Haitian and a little spooked."

She chuckled. "I guess that's why Emmitt is so docile."

Chuckling with her, he said, "No, dear, he's just . . . stupid."

"I guess there isn't much expected of you here."

"Honey, this is Florida; there are no expectations."

They both laughed, and over the next few hours, they became father and daughter once again. Since he had been reading the paper, there was little he didn't know about the neighbors. It was the boys and her and her husband that enthralled him as she gave him as much information as she could quickly recall.

It was toward the end that it came out. She hadn't wanted to say it at this time; it just appeared, and it surprised her when it spilled out, dart-like.

"Why did you leave?"

He didn't seem surprised at the question. A shade of relief crossed his face, and his eyes seemed to lighten a little.

"I guess you're owed an explanation," he said as he nervously massaged his palm with his thumb. "When your brother died," he began in a steady, rehearsed tone, "it was very difficult for me to get past it. It was my fault. I should have adjusted the brake tighter, or turned off the engine, or something that could've prevented it from happening." He stopped, and a grey shade of regret and grief filled his cheeks as his eyes reddened with the memory. "As long as I live, I will remember picking him up," he stretched out his arms, his eyes glaring through them as if the child's body was once again between them, "and carrying him to the house, and going inside and laying him on the couch. I could still feel his warmth through my hands, but I knew he was gone. Whenever he was close, even when he was sick, he would always try to hold my hand. Now his hands just dangled."

He stopped, breaking the trance, and stared at her.

"How do you get past that?" he asked rhetorically. "It became obvious that from the glances of the neighbors, my friends, the looks of distrust from your mother whenever I was around you, the pity of my parents—I realized if I were to stay there in that small town, I would never get over it. That none of us would. I thought the best thing for all of us . . . was for me to leave."

For a few moments, the only sound was the clatter of rolling luggage, the occasional overhead announcement. She didn't know what to say.

"Every day, I think of it, and I think of him."

"It was selfish," she said quietly, brushing away the tear running over her cheek.

"Maybe. Because I don't feel any different now than I did when it happened."

The exchange was becoming uncomfortable, and she began to shift awkwardly.

"How long are you staying?" he asked quietly.

"I'm taking the last plane out tomorrow so I can be home by Sunday and get the boys off to school Monday morning."

"Would you like to go out tonight to get some dinner or something?" he asked, his voice trailing away at the end.

"Actually, I would like to just check into my hotel and lay on the bed for a while." She paused. "I'm not sure what to do or what to say." She stood up unsteadily and bent over to give him a soft hug.

He nodded and stared at the vacant chair as she walked to the desk, collected her belongings, and walked through the terminal toward her waiting rental car.

Reaching the hotel, she stumbled through the checkout line, sweltering in her thick clothes as the Florida humidity engulfed her. Emotions of grief and longing washed over her in waves as she hoped for some shred of deliverance, some open door that could pull her out of the waves of misery she had willingly entered.

In the shower, her tears mixed with water as she cleansed the dirt and sweat away. Walking into her room, she didn't dress and instead slipped under the covers of the bed, surrounding herself with the darkness of the draped room.

Images of her childhood with and without him sorted through her mind like flipping index cards on a rolodex. Images of when he should have been there—the dances, the homecomings, the softball games, and hayrides—made her clench her fists in regret and anger. The broken hearts she had to endure alone when she needed a strong shoulder. The driving lessons he failed to teach, the pitches he never threw, the walks they never took. Wanting to scream at him in anger and rage wasn't possible, so she sobbed until the pillow casing was soaked in tears.

Gradually it began to lessen, and the emotion began to abate. Hungry, she ordered a cheeseburger and a liter of tonic water. Responding to the knock on the door, she quickly threw on her jeans and a sweatshirt and opened it to see a thin Hispanic with soft brown eyes presenting her with a tray of food.

"Thank you," she said as she took it from him. "I'll just take it from here."

"Is there anything else?" the boy asked politely.

"Yes," she said. "I need some gin."

"I'm sorry. I cannot bring that to your room, and the hotel does not have a bar."

"I see," she said. "I believe that's your fifty on the floor."

Looking down at his feet, he saw fifty-dollar bill folded diagonally.

Taken aback at first, he quickly gathered the inference and smiled a half smile as his eyes darkened with the danger of the felony opportunity.

Picking it up quickly, he slipped it into his pocket.

"I'll be back in thirty minutes." He slipped away down the hall and around the corner with big strides.

True to his word, a knock sounded once again twenty-six minutes later, and when she opened the door, there was a crumpled brown bag at her feet, its sides smoothed by the shape of the bottle and its carrier disappearing down the hall with a flash of a black shoe and a streak of burgundy jacket. She smiled as she gripped the bag and imagined her change was in it.

Throughout the night, she sipped gin and tonics. The regrets and disappointments were deep and bitter, and she easily vented them, but as these percolated away, there was a calmness seeping through. There was a layer, a bedrock of good memories that was quietly attaching itself to the strands of contempt. Memories of state fairs and family dinners and quiet family nights on the porch with Dad trying to play the harmonica, Mom sitting on the porch and gazing at the horizon and the stars, while the children caught lightning bugs and slapped them into empty wide-mouth mayonnaise jars. As she ran in the cool night air, she would struggle through her fatigue to trap them until her father finally called them inside for the night.

In the stillness of her childhood room, she remembered his goodnight kiss, the tender wave of his hand over her head and face, and the quiet promise of "Tomorrow's another day" as he closed the door. Forever images that pushed through the doubt like pillars—firm, profound, and towering.

The night grew deeper, her tears dried, and a resolute in her heart formed, clear and pronounced. Sluggishly, she slipped out of bed, drank a last swallow from the bathroom glass, and clucked her teeth. The glass settled loudly on the desk, the sheets rustled stiffly, and soon the gin settled her into an uneasy sleep.

The next morning, she shook off the hangover with a few aspirin and a tall glass of orange juice. The bagels at the continental breakfast in the conference room by the main entrance looked a little too rough and the eggs too risky. Settling on a bran muffin, she nibbled it slowly as the early morning warmth seeped into the hallway. Choosing a table by the large picture window, she watched a small, brown lizard struggle to crawl from under a leaf and rest at the foot of a palm tree to gather as much of the morning sun's warmth.

"I wish it was that easy," she said as she ate slowly, allowing the last sway of alcohol to seep from her limbs and for some reason to alleviate the numbness in her teeth.

As the morning progressed, the edges of her emotions dulled, and the choices seemed more certain and clear. In the afternoon, she drove to a nearby beach and let the sun and salt air cleanse the last of her thoughts. She never entered the water—she wasn't much for swimming—but watched the people as they strolled at the water's edge or played in the sand with their families. Her mind was becoming strangely clear, as if that part of her brain had guarded itself from the booze, knowing that it had to coalesce all of her thoughts. The principles she had discovered before she fell asleep came back clearly to her in the words of trust, love, respect, and from these came her only conclusion—forgiveness.

Within an hour after returning to her room, she had her bags packed and had taken a cab back to the airport. Routinely, she dropped her keys to the attendant, took her suitcases, and walked into the terminal. Stopping at a pay phone, she phoned home to a relieved Dale and told him she was on her way home and would be there as planned. Placing the receiver back softly, she shifted her purse to her strong shoulder and wheeled the suitcase over to the terminal desk to get her tickets and to page her father to tell him she was going back home but would return as soon as she could.

Emmitt was the only one at the desk, bowed over a manifest, oblivious to her approach until the soft tap of her finger drew his attention. Stopping abruptly, he stared at her in guarded anticipation.

"Could you please page my father? I would like to say good-bye to him."

"Um," Emmitt stuttered, not really sure how to respond, the truth suddenly slipping out like a overflowing sink. "He quit yesterday." Suddenly remembering his instructions, he leapt to the other side of the desk and began fumbling with a stack of papers.

Shocked, she didn't know how to respond except with "Oh." Suddenly everything she had presumed in the morning, teased out at night, and had resolved in a gin-drunk state seemed forlorn and wasted.

"But he left this for you," Emmitt said as he shifted the oversized shirt to a little higher on his shoulder.

Cautiously, she reached out and took the plain white envelope Emmitt was offering. It was unsealed, and when she had slipped the heavy paper away, she stared at a black and white photograph of an old man with no teeth holding a brilliant yellow flower. There were no words on the cover, and she opened it slowly to a simple sentence written in heartbreakingly familiar script.

"I want to come home if you'll have me" was all it said.

Her eyes welled up as she tried to make out the small script word seemingly written as an afterthought rather than a signature—Dad.

She looked away to prevent a tear from landing on the paper and saw him standing by the bench they had talked on the day before, neatly dressed in dated, clean pants and a crisp, white shirt. He was holding a very small bag.

"It was the only card they had that I thought would work." He smiled shyly, and she quietly returned his smile, slipped her arm into his, and led him to the ticket counter and the waiting flight home.

Adrienne's letter

— •• —

EASING THE RUSTED LATE-MODEL SEDAN to the side of the road in front of the rented house, Bobby slipped the transmission into park. Sliding the last inch of a cigar out of his mouth, he flicked off the ash in the general direction of a small, black ashtray glued to the center of the dashboard. Located directly overhead were two donkey air-fresheners, with the animal grinning broadly back over its butt and the sentence "Kiss My Ass" in broad white hillbilly script. With his free hand, he gave the horn two quick shots and slid the cigar back between his lips, where it hung as he squinted at a dimly-lit front door just off in the distance.

Rolling it in his mouth from corner to corner, the unlit stub was as lifeless as the cool August night. The street had no lights, and the thin beams of his late-model car showed nothing but bare, cracked asphalt bordered by seldom mowed weeds two feet high. Occasionally, a moth would flicker across, fluttering its way toward one of the dilapidated shacks that passed as residences along the street. A thin rain was beginning to fall, and the sweet smell of fresh water on pavement still warm from the heat of the day gave a distinctly fresh aroma to a badly worn section of town.

Typically a patient man, he never minded waiting. Adrienne always took her time getting to the car. They were never in much of a hurry to go to the empty lot by the distribution center and smoke dope, but tonight her frenzied call ordered him to come over right away.

Stumbling out of his second-story, one-bedroom apartment in the two-apartment building he shared with his mother, he had grabbed a too tight jacket, which he struggled to get on as he fumbled his way down the stairs. After searching frantically for the right key in the thin dome light of the car, he had grasped the hub of the key and shoved it in the ignition while turning the switch. The car roared to life, its engine as tightly maintained as the exterior was neglected, and pulled away as quickly as possible. By using his left foot on the brake and his right on the gas, he had been able to stop-start his way through a half-dozen stop signs and one yield as he wildly traversed the ten miles of unincorporated roads to Adrienne's house.

Now he waited, a little anxious as he stared out the window, looking for some sign of life to pass from the robin's egg blue door on the lime green house. With his left hand, he held the wheel tightly, while with his right, he drummed on the strips of wrinkled duct tape that stretched over the tears in the fake leather seat.

When she burst through the door, he almost jumped with surprise. Having just returned home from her job as a waitress at the Pilgrim Waffle house in the center of town, she was still clad in the burgundy uniform with a white apron across the front. Purple and red splotches adorned the apron, remnants of plates removed. Around it, she had covered herself with her pink bathrobe, and she held a thick envelope over her head as protection against the thickening rain.

As he watched her dash down the broken sidewalk, jumping over the puddles beginning to form in the low areas, he could hear the slapping of her bare feet on the concrete growing louder as she approached the car door. With a quick rush of wind, she bolted through it, slamming it shut so hard behind her that the jingle of loose bolts in the door continued to roll around. The fresh mist of air was sweet with rain and was mixed quickly with the scents of maple syrup and coffee. Breathing heavily, her hair slowly melting over her brow from the weight of the rain, she stared at him wild-eyed and short of breath.

Having never seen her this way before, he moved uneasily, took the stub from his mouth, and tossed it out the cracked side window.

"What's going on, honey bear?" he asked unsteadily, dreadfully awaiting the sudden display of an EPT test stick and the pink tag of certain bondage.

She said nothing. Continuing to breathe hard, she extended her hand with a damp envelope, reaching it out slowly until her arm was straight and the letter was almost flat against his chest.

Smiling faintly, he glanced quickly at the letterhead and breathed a short sigh of relief, seeing that it was from the postal service and not a doctor or lawyer. Delicately, he took from her the government's apology letter and a dusty, white envelope. Glancing at the post office script, he shrugged and smiled at her. "It's the government, baby. They fuck everything up."

"Open the card," she blurted out. "You have to open the card!"

Slipping his hand into the large envelope, he pulled out a Christmas card with the jovial smile of a glittered Saint Nicholas and an equally adorned, cherubic Rudolph standing obediently beside him. As the card cleared the envelope, two blue, thin lottery game cards slid out of the bottom and landed in his lap.

Laying the card, letter, and envelope on the dashboard, he glanced at the two tickets in front of him. It was a simple game—scratch off the spaces and try to match three numbers. If you do, you win the amount. Being lottery holiday cards, there were images of elves and reindeer and a couple of snowmen dancing and rejoicing with money being thrown in the air. Money just there for the taking. None of them had been touched, and the cardboard they were printed on was hard and brittle.

"Play them," she said and slipped a dime into his hand.

"But these are for you."

"Then for me, play them."

He shrugged, and with broad sweeping motions, he cleared away the erasable rubber, revealing denominations of $10, $100, $500, $1000, and so forth all the way up to even higher denominations. In the seconds it took to discover if he was a winner, he rapidly learned he had lost. Smiling, he turned to her and chuckled slightly.

"Sorry, babe, I guess I'm just not lucky enough for you."

She stared at him blankly. The rain dripping down from her hair began to mingle with a tear appearing at the corner of her eye.

Caught off guard, he stopped laughing and rapidly reviewed everything he had done and said so he could apologize appropriately, quickly, and sincerely.

"I'm sorry, baby. I didn't realize it was that important to you." He reached out with a coarse palm in an attempt to push away her hair and wipe away the tear. Intercepting his reach, he felt another lottery card slip between his fingers. Bewildered, he glanced at the face of it, the neatly erased squares cleared completely with the exception of one in the lower right hand corner. But he didn't notice that error as much as the three silver and blue $10,000 numbers shimmering back at him in the thin light of the cab.

"Only one winner per person," she said as she smiled and wiped away her tears of joy. "This one's mine."

The lottery ticket was from Texas, roughly 800 miles from the southern Illinois town where the letter was received. The closest lottery office where they could claim the money was in Texarkana. Adrienne was able to get other waitresses to cover her late afternoon shift, but only for four days, as Madeline was quitting to join up with her husband on the carnival circuit. Since Bobby was doing odd jobs, he wouldn't be missed. They had to leave early in the morning, and they did, piling into a borrowed pickup truck's cab at the sharp rise of the sun. Taking the small, flowered suitcase from Adrienne, he placed it in the back of the rusted bed, right up next to the cab between his duffel and his steel toolbox. Turning the truck around in the road, it almost choked dead on the gas from the effort Bobby demanded of it, but the truck recovered quickly, and they pulled out on the road leading to the main access to Route 31, and from there to Interstate 55. Adrienne looked back through the oil-stained rear window and toward her home fading in the distance.

The eastern sun was beginning to illuminate the small patchwork of houses and mobile homes collected around gravel driveways and cracked concrete pads. Tall thickets of weeds glistened with the morning light, still holding the rain from the night before. They gave a sense of fragility against the hardwood of trashed machines, rotten cars, and abandoned furniture.

Behind her wasn't a dying landscape, just one gasping for a chance to have an identity. Subdivision or farm field—pick one.

They promised each other they would eat only a little breakfast—whatever was left from the pop tart box or donut bag—hit a drive-through for lunch, and actually sit down for dinner. The single credit card he had didn't allow much, and the conversation with the bank representative didn't persuade them to raise the amount above $500 despite his assurances that he was going to collect a huge payout at the lottery office.

The first day went exceptionally well. The weather was great, they got along very well, and nothing of any significance fell off of the truck.

Reaching the outskirts of St. Louis, they passed through and decided to settle in at a small motel with the promise of a clean bed and cable. Not much more. A diner graced the front entrance. Thin on drapes and strong on steel tables, they settled into a brilliant red booth with the least amount of stuffing bleeding out of the worn seats. They scanned the plastic coated menu with the entrees neatly typed and organized on the page. A small, red sheet of paper slipped out of his and slid halfway across the table. Glancing at it briefly, he slid it toward Adrienne and resumed looking at the menu.

With a light crowd in the restaurant, the waitress was quick to drop off glasses of water, remark that the meatloaf had just come out of the oven, take their orders, and slip away.

For a few seconds, they sat there and smiled at each other, awkward in a dining luxury they never afforded themselves—eating out.

Leaning forward, a devilish look in his eye, he whispered softly to her, "So, where did you hide the ticket?"

She leaned forward, returning his smile. "I have it taped to my back," she whispered back.

"I'll have to get it out for you later." He grinned.

"You can try, but I don't think Aunt Renee would approve of you using her holiday gift as a way to get my clothes off."

"Was that who the card was from?" he remarked, suddenly losing his desire for mischief.

"Uh-huh," she answered. "After I turned eighteen, she sent me lottery tickets every Christmas."

"I don't remember you getting one last year," Bobby remarked.

"I didn't get one last year, but I figured she was just too sick. Remember, she died in February."

Feeling the need to explain further, she took a long drink of water and continued.

"See, Aunt Renee didn't really have anyone. She had two nephews with no kids of her own. One was my dad, and the other was Uncle Ricky. As you know, my dad died a while ago, when I was twelve, and Uncle Ricky lived in Mississippi and worked on the oil rigs in the gulf, so he would be gone for months at a time."

"So there was nobody close?"

"No. I think the neighbors kept an eye on her though. It was one of them that called and told us she had died."

"So you didn't get anything else from her or go to the funeral?"

She hesitated. "No, I don't think we got anything 'cause there wasn't anything. When the first cards came, I never even knew I had an Aunt Renee. When I asked my mom who she was and where she lived so I could visit her and thank her, she just said it was dad's relation and she lived in one of the those old hotels in Texas where there was only one room and like the bed folded up against the wall."

Bobby frowned a little at the mechanics of how a bed would fold up against a wall but let it pass as Adrienne continued her story.

"Mom said all she really had was social security, and I was lucky to get six dollars' worth of tickets, as she barely had enough to feed her and her cats."

"That's always annoyed me." Bobby interjected, crossing his arms over his chest. "Why does somebody who doesn't have any money still have pets that they take care of? It's very confusing to me."

Adrienne shrugged. "Maybe she thought that if times got real bad, she could eat them."

Bobby smiled at the thought. As if on cue, the food arrived, a double portion of meatloaf and mashed potatoes for Bobby, and a fish sandwich and fries for Adrienne.

"Anything else?" the waitress asked, slipping a new bottle of ketchup out of her apron and onto the table next to Bobby. Like a shadow, a small Hispanic busboy dropped off two sodas and faded away.

Shaking their heads no, they quickly unrolled their silverware from the taped napkins, and the waitress whipped out her order pad and headed toward new customers that were taking seats two booths away.

Vigorously, Bobby sprinkled the salt and then the pepper over the steaming brown meat. Leaning toward her as he assembled his knife and fork, he said softly under his breath, "Here, kitty, kitty."

With a mouthful of fish sandwich, she quickly covered her lips with the back of her hand, turning a sharp laugh into a heavy snort.

Laughing to themselves, they quickly devoured their only true meal of the day and readily took advantage of the free coffee and ice cream available afterwards.

The next morning, the sun was bright. Its beams reflected off the windshields and aluminum roof of the hotel in a brilliant scream. Even the small, heavily chlorinated pool looked new and enticing.

With their thin collection of valuables in hand, Adrienne walked out to the truck, her hand trying to screen the rays as she tossed her bag in the back and jumped into the passenger side. Bobby slammed her door hard, walked around the pickup, and did the same on the driver's side.

On the fourth rotation of the key, the engine roared to life and then settled into a thick, smoking pulse.

First, they stopped at the motel office to settle the bill, grab a handful of donuts, and two Styrofoam cups of coffee. Ten minutes later, the truck was on the interstate again heading south on a clear highway.

The early morning sun was warm, and it felt soothing as Adrienne slipped off her shoes and placed her bare feet on the glove box. The rumbling from the engine gravitated into the dashboard, and the subtle vibrations gave her an odd sense of security. Like being on a stead that knows the way, her trust came blindly. Taking a small sip of her coffee, she let the combination of all things good settle into her body and soul, and closed her eyes in silent reverence.

"What color's that?" Bobby asked.

Crossing her brow in annoyance, she glared at him with one open eye.

"What?" she asked sharply.

"Your toenails. What kind of color is that? It looks like red, but it's not."

"It's called pumpkin sunrise."

"Doesn't look orange either."

"It's supposed to be both."

"Doesn't look like it's either one. Doesn't seem to work too well."

She closed her eye and pushed herself deeper into the seat. "Works for me," she mumbled.

"Damn!" he exclaimed, glancing at the Shrek clock figurine stuck to the violet-blue dashboard. "We're making great time! We'll be there and back home before anyone knows we're gone."

She didn't even bother to give his chance at conversation any notice. She just let the silence kill it.

The second attempt she had to address, if only because it intrigued her.

"Have you thought about what you're going to do with the money?" he asked.

Slowly raising her head, she opened her eyes and watched the light poles flip past in a perfectly timed sequence.

"No," she lied.

"Well, not to tell you what to do, but if I were you, I'd look at maybe getting a new car. I've worked on some really old ones that are in great shape, and I know I could get you a great deal on one—and I'll work on it for free so that you'll never have to worry about it breaking down or anything."

"If it's such a good car, why would it break down?" she asked calmly.

"Well . . . shit happens."

She sighed and adjusted the grey T-shirt she was wearing so the sleeves were even. Thinking very carefully, she turned to look out the window as the truck sped over a bridge that spanned a small intersection. Below, she could see two gas stations, a convenience store next to a small budget hotel, and a diner similar to where she worked. A reminder of what she was going back to once she had the money.

"I want to use the money to change my life," she answered finally. "There has got to be something else in this world other than hoping that old, fat Dolores Keenan will get her full Social Security check so she can quit and I can get her first shift spot so I'm not third shift until four o'clock in the god-damn morning. Have you seen her shoulders, Bobby?" Adrienne asked, glancing at him as he gave a loose shrug. "She's bent over terribly, and they're," she formed the shape with her hands, "round and soft." She paused and looked out the window. "It's from all those dishes and trays and glasses. It wears you down. I don't want to be worn down, Bobby."

"What do you mean . . . like change your life?" he asked.

"I mean just . . ." she struggled a little for the words, the right phase, the perfect sentence, " . . . just take it and go."

"Go where?"

"I don't know. Maybe I'll take the money and go to school, or open up my own little shop, or just . . ." And there she ended it.

"Maybe you could get new furniture for your place or something like that."

She turned and glared at him, at the pillar of stupidity he had become.

"Maybe I'll take the money and marry your butt. Maybe I'll take the money and flash it in front of you and say, 'Are you in or out? Are you going to marry me, or just spend the rest of your life in your mom's basement playing your ninja games all god-damn night long, which accomplishes absolutely nothing?'" Realizing she was almost shouting, she took a deep breath and crossed her arms.

In a vain attempt at a defense, he set his jaw and moved his hands awkwardly around the steering wheel. "It helps strengthen my hands so I can do my job better."

"I think it just makes your thumbs longer so you can stick them up your ass further."

An emotional chasm had now opened . . . widely. This he knew not from his intellect and keen perception of the human spirit, but because of the Christmases where she waited for the ring that never came, because of the first-date anniversaries that were becoming stale and old, having never turned into wedding anniversaries, and because the shear routine of their life was getting burdensome. For a fleeting moment he thought that maybe it was time. Things should go forward; perhaps marriage was the door he should walk through. Then it suddenly became apparent to him. As clear as he had ever noticed. The key he was given in the third world of his Black

Knight game opened the hidden latch underneath the chest because it wasn't a chest at all, but a door to another level in the Dragon's Castle. Of course, it was so obvious; now he just had to get through the company of gnomes. He'd address this as soon as he got home.

Adrienne glanced over and noticed a look of revelation and discovery on his face. He almost seemed to be beaming, and she drew a deep breath and smiled to herself at the chance, the hope, that he finally understood.

When they were within thirty miles of the Texas border, Bobby pulled over at an off-ramp that was a little more densely packed than the others they had driven by. In addition to the two gas stations, motel, and diner, there was also a small video shop, another full-sized restaurant, a beauty/barber shop, and a store selling authentic Chinese fireworks.

While Bobby got out and filled the tank, stuffing his hands into his pockets and looking longingly at the fireworks store, Adrienne reached behind her and felt the sharp corner of the lottery ticket's cardboard. Assured that it was still firmly taped to her back, she reached into her front pocket, watching Bobby all the while. As Bobby's staring at the fireworks store turned more seductive, she slipped the quarter-folded piece of paper out and glanced at the man's name and phone number hastily scratched along the edge. *Mark 886-2154* was all it said, but she looked at it hard and long, until she heard the thud of the gas latch closing and the slip of the nozzle going back onto the pump. When Bobby returned to the driver's seat, he flashed her a quick smile, which she readily returned, knowing that the paper was securely buried deep in her front pants pocket.

After pulling into Texarkana, they spent a few hours driving around trying to get their bearings. They eventually found the lottery office and pulled into the small parking lot next to the low, single-story brick building. Bobby had changed from the grey sweatpants and oversized T-shirt he had been wearing into a nice pair of faded blue jeans and a horribly wrinkled white shirt. Adrienne had also changed and was wearing a peach blouse and knee-length blue jean skirt. She had removed the lottery ticket from its hiding place on her lower back and now held it tightly in her right hand.

Bobby had reached out with his right to get her left, and together they walked hand in hand up the front steps. Pushing through the heavy wooden doors with thick-paneled wire glass, they walked into a great room with a series of wall desks on the right side, floor posts delineating lines in the center, and a long clerical desk on the left with a number of white-shirted clerks behind them. The air conditioning cooled the sweat in her right hand, and she felt a chill, and the nerves twitched in response. She suddenly wondered if the moisture from her palm would wash away or blur the numbers, feeding the continual fear that none of this could be happening. But she doubled down on her grip on the card, and its brittleness reassured her it was real and going nowhere.

Walking directly through the thin crowd, they picked the shallowest line and waited all of ten minutes before they were standing in front of a tall man with thick glasses and a sheepish grin. With a deep breath, she slid the lottery card face down toward him, Bobby recoiling slightly as she gripped his hand in an unconsciously tightening move. For the first time, she noticed what he had been saying all along—his thumbs were bigger and more muscular.

With a sharp blink, the clerk took the card, bringing it up close to his eyes to examine it in great detail. His look of concern caused her heart to skip as he took the card to a middle-aged woman seated two rows behind the counter. Handing the card over to her, he then whispered to her, and she in turn knitted her brow.

On her desk was a small black box attacked to a scanning gun. With the touch of an expert, she scraped away a series of numbers at the bottom of the card with her fingernail, blowing away the filings as she went. Once all of the numbers were exposed, she pulled out the scanner from its carriage and momentarily held it over the card like a hawk soaring over a mouse in a ditch.

With a loud beep and a flash of red light, the scanner acknowledged the ticket. Adrienne unknowingly dropped Bobby's hand, lacing both hands over her mouth as the process worked to its completion. Her heart was racing as the clerk walked over to an electronic printer that was whirling madly. In the meantime, the woman stood up from her desk and walked toward Adrienne, a printed white form in her hand.

"I need some specific information," she said, and in a voice surprisingly strong, Adrienne answered all of the questions relating to address, date of birth, social security number, and other bureaucratic identifiers. By chance, as she finished the last questions, the first clerk walked over holding a long envelope-sized check with the number $10,000 printed in thick black letters and the receiver signature line left open.

"You spell your last name D-i-l-l-i-o-n?" She then asked for some positive verification. Dumbfounded by the amount, Adrienne only nodded. With the push of a black pen she seemed to produce from nowhere, the woman wrote Adrienne's name across the receiver's slip line with a large sweeping motion. Deftly reaching under the counter, she produced a small red stamp. Initialing the end of the line, she formalized it with a sharp crack of the stamp, sealing the initial with a small reddish mark.

Reaching under the counter one last time, she switched the stamp for an envelope, which she then placed underneath the check. Sliding the papers toward Adrienne, the woman said congratulations in a soft voice, smiled faintly with the formality of an everyday exchange, and then turned to walk back to her desk to finish what she had started.

The clerk, now smiling to reveal two busted teeth and a line brown from coffee stains, leaned forward. "I think I love you," he revealed and followed it with a slight chuckle.

Suddenly giddy with a ticket now turned to gold, she laughed a little, followed by a sudden snort, as Bobby gave him a lean eye, grabbed Adrianne's hand, and walked her out of the building, smiling.

As luck would have it, there was a popular bank on the corner, and they bee-lined toward it. Twenty minutes later, they had opened a checking account and pocketed $100 for lunch.

With the money now secure, a heavy burden was lifted, and a deep hunger set in. As they started to head back toward the highway, they found a nice restaurant with outdoor tables that took full advantage of the afternoon sun. Getting seated quickly, they ordered two light beers, and as the waitress left, they looked at each other and smiled.

Adrienne closed her eyes and felt the sun on her face, her mind wandering into eddies of thought while Bobby stared at the bubbles forming slowly and then drifting to the top in his beer, wondering where they came from and where they go.

"I feel like this huge curtain has been lifted from around my head, and I can see off into the distance, and it's all gold."

She opened her eyes and stared out at the dirty cars that drove past. "Just like Willy Wonka, I have the gold ticket to all the candy."

"Well, really, he didn't win anything."

Adrienne glared at him as he made a line with his thumb through the condensation on the side of the glass.

"See," he continued, "it wasn't Willy Wonka, he already owned the factory, it was Charlie who got the gold ticket, and he didn't win anything. In fact, I think he gave it back."

"He flew away in the helicopter through the roof of the factory with the guy." Adrienne struggled a little now, trying to remember the story. "You know the guy in the purple suit—"

"Yeah," Bobby interjected. "Willy Wonka. And the only reason he was in the helicopter was because he was the least annoying of all the rotten kids that were there." Bobby leaned back in his chair, placing his hands on his jeans, revealing the unfastened top button of his pants. "Just because you're the least terrible of only a few kids doesn't mean you win; it just means you're the least terrible. Christ, one kid got turned into a frickin' blueberry and got drained."

Bobby crinkled his face at the thought of the effort and machinery required to do the procedure. "Man, that's a cold dude."

Somewhere in Adrienne's mind, as she stared at the man-boy across from her, a glimpse of the future appeared. A future of promising hopes and plans tethered together like so many barges, only now the knots were slipping, and the frayed ropes were separating softly. The barges were slowly fading down the river aimlessly. Left to their own devices, they had no guide, and now they only drifted apart. The man that she had known, and cried for, and hoped for, for six years, was seated there before her—and she truly, honestly looked at him. And then amongst the hallways and chambers in the theater of her consciousness, another curtain fell, only this one didn't show a revelation or exhibit an emotional release but supplied an ending. The applause had drifted away, the play was over, lower the curtain. Fade to black.

"Man, you know, I have a serious problem with that movie too. I mean, you put a kid in a chocolate river, he's going to try and drink the whole thing. That's just being a kid—I mean, what'd you expect? Man, I would have dove into it; you would have never seen me again."

Suddenly realizing that she was rubbing her front pocket, she abruptly stopped and folded her hands on the table as Bobby continued on about living on chocolate, dwarves, and how creepy it is for all the grandparents to be sleeping in the same bed.

They made good time getting home, and as a thanks to Bobby, she slipped him a check to cover his expenses and a little more.

"I knew you were good for it," he jokingly remarked as he dropped her off at her house and did his usual U-turn to head back to the highway.

Settling back into her sullen, overflowing, two-bedroom home, she glanced at her watch and decided now was as good a time as any. Slipping her fingers into her jeans, she felt the corner of the paper and slowly pulled it out. It was deeply wrinkled now, the numbers fading slightly from the abrasiveness of the denim. But she laid it on the counter by the kitchen phone and smoothed it out repeatedly with her hand, hoping to build confidence with the touch. Making it routine instead of original.

Taking a deep breath, and then faintly breathing, she punched the numbers in and then listened as the phone purred three times.

"Absolutely Travel. How may we direct your call?" a woman answered.

"May I speak to Mark please?"

"Just one second, let me check," the woman answered, murmuring slightly over a hand-shielded receiver and then returning with a strong voice. "He's here. Let me send you over to his desk."

The phone clicked and then purred only once before a young man's voice spoke. "This is Mark. How can I help you?"

"Hi, Mark. It's Adrienne."

"Do I know you?" he asked.

"No," she replied hesitantly. "But I got your number from a friend, and she said you were really nice and everything, and she really liked you."

"Okay." She could tell he was smiling on the end of the line. "What can I do for you?"

"I need a ticket somewhere, anywhere, but it needs to be far and exotic . . . and one-way."

Sal's letter

———— •❖• ————

SALVATORE "THE CHEMIST" CALVINI STARED at the reflection in his bedroom dresser mirror one last time. He adjusted the collar on his pressed, heavily starched, white shirt, leaving the top button open to reveal the slender gold chain around his neck, yet hiding the thin cross that rested comfortably against his chest. He liked his shirts heavily starched because they held their creases over his long days, and the coarseness made him feel like he was wearing a suit of armor.

He was rough on shirts, so they seldom lasted a few months anyway. It was torn or stained long before the starch had eaten away the threads. Vincent's Men's Clothing had a standing order to deliver three shirts the first of every month. It was an order that had existed for twenty years, with only one size change in all that time. The best part of the convenience was the cost. No money exchanged, only the perpetual return of a favor long ago rendered.

He slicked back the thin, black hair along the side of his head, slightly greased to keep it in place, yet not overly slicked back. Doing that in his youth made his perfectly round head look like a billiard ball. "Eight-Ball Sal," one guy tried to call him. He said it once, and only once. The guy then became "Two-Straws Torelli" because that was all the man could put in his mouth for six months as his pulverized jaw was wired shut.

Convinced he had the look set, he glanced at the man he had become. At fifty-six, he was a successful businessman that had established a solid presence at the railroad yard. All commerce coming in and out was under his thumb. All the men in the cranes and behind the trucks reported to him. At fifty-six, he didn't look the part, a quiet and unassuming face, a slight paunch, but rounded shoulders and the arms of a linebacker. All of his hair had receded from the brow to the back of the neck, but it gave him a sense of physical maturity he never had as a young man.

Taking a deep breath, he turned to the bed behind him and picked up his brown sport coat. He slipped it over his shoulders and pulled the lapel straight with a snap. He then turned back to the mirror and gathered his possessions from the top of his dresser, placing them in the appropriate pockets. Keys in the front right, lighter in the front left—he never smoked, but he knew many who did. White handkerchief in the right rear pants pocket, a small folded envelope in the left rear billfold inside the front of the sport coat, tarnished and nicked brass knuckles in the lower left outside pocket, cell phone in the shirt breast pocket.

Fully outfitted, he left the small bedroom of the apartment, walked through the living room and to the kitchen on the other side, thereby completing a full tour of his residence. Opening a slender upper cabinet, he pulled out a clear mayonnaise jar. He unscrewed it, took out a small packet of powder heavily sealed in plastic wrap, placed it in the middle of his handkerchief, and returned it to his back pocket. He left the apartment, walked the two flights of wide stairs covered in aged red velvet, and passed through the front door and into a waiting cab.

"Same place?" the driver asked without turning to look, concentrating instead on getting back into the nearest lane after a thick clot of cars had passed.

"Yeah," Sal answered as he slid to the middle of the rear seat.

Easing the wheel over, the driver guided the car to an opening between a red Civic and a city bus, and then let the wheel slide back to center between his hands as the car entered the traffic artery. Comfortable with the pace and speed, he then peered into the rearview mirror to examine his passenger.

"You're looking pretty healthy today, Mr. Sal," he chimed.

"Thank you, Aldo," Sal responded.

Sal glanced back at the driver's reflection, a very familiar one at that. For the hundredth time in the last few years, he saw the youthful, round, bearded face be-speckled with thick lenses on rounded, dark frames. The driver's long, thick, curly hair tracked over small rounded shoulders, capped with a red beret pitched to one side. It was very much like looking at a red canopy on top of an ash mountain.

"What's up with the fucking hat?" Sal blurted out, smiling at the anticipated reply.

"It's a beret, Mr. Sal," the driver responded in a suddenly soprano voice, almost child-like.

"A beret? What's it supposed to do? Doesn't look like it will keep the rain out or cover up that fishnet you call hair."

"Well actually, it's my new look. See, me and Lucia split up, and I'm looking for a new girl. Somebody smarter—you know, somebody who I can talk to on a higher level."

"Really!" Sal shouted in mock amusement. "You two finally split up for sure?"

"Oh, absolutely!" he replied as he made a left turn against the light, honked the horn, flipped off a pedestrian, and centered the car in the middle lane. "I know we split up a bunch of times before and always got back together, but this time it's different . . . I mean, I'm definitely not going back!" He jabbed his thick finger at the rearview mirror to make his point.

"I see," Sal replied.

"In fact, I now carry a book around with me to perhaps reflect on the intellectual thinkings I have."

Without looking over, he reached to the passenger seat and displayed a thick leather-bound book. Sal had to squint to see the lettering on the spine.

"Mr. Aldo!" Sal retorted. "What you have in your hand is an encyclopedia. The letters T through U, I believe."

"Exactly!" Aldo replied. "Smart people read books with facts in them."

"Did you start with A?"

"No, just this one. I like turtles, and it has lots of turtle pictures in it."

"I see," was all Sal could muster as a reply.

"I figure once the assumption of my intellect is assumed," Aldo began, allowing the book to drop into the seat next to him, the pages slapping together like a loud clap, "the rest of me will seem inconsequential and unimportant."

"Well, good luck with that!" Sal stated with a strong push of support, followed by a roll of the eyes and a sly grin.

Looking out the window, his attention now turned to the small stores and people they were passing. The storefronts were bringing up names that were snapping by like a flipping deck of cards, more image than identity. Having lived in this neighborhood his whole life, he knew all of these people and places. There were storeowners that were still here because of him, and they were all grateful, returning their gratitude in endless favors without complaint. "Use your influence in your neighborhood," his old boss, Frankie "The Pipe" Vichusi used to say. "These people will make your bones. When they respect you, they will watch your back because you are one of them." Frankie was the best. The father who stayed to replace the father who had left. Sal learned a lot from him; he made Sal who he was today.

Rolling to a stop at a light just two intersections away from the restaurant, Sal peered down the street and felt a sudden sadness. The feeling came and went as it chose, but it seemed to show up most often at this intersection. It was here that he was with another driver and listening to the radio when the newsman mentioned the beating death of the notorious mob boss Frankie Vichusi in prison. No one was ever charged with the murder, just another gangland slaying according to the police, meaning it would never be pursued, never solved.

But it was as much a mystery to him as it was to the police. Typically there was a reason why—a debt to pay, a message to be sent, a proof of loyalty. This time, there was nothing. Sal even called in his own informants, interviewing every one, trying to learn who okayed the contract. But no one knew who made the authorization, and if they did, there was a much greater fear of that person than there was of Sal and his influence. But now Sal had an assumption. A hunch, and a pretty good one. He had a plan, and he hoped it would work; he just needed the proof. Tapping the pocket where his handkerchief was bundled, he felt secure that it wouldn't fail.

"Thinking of Frankie?" Aldo broke the silence as the car rolled forward. "There isn't a day that goes by that I don't think of him too."

Sal didn't know how to respond, but he didn't have to as the car rolled up to the curb in front of a small diner with the marquee "Louie's" towering vertically over the small windowed frontage.

The cab had scarcely stopped when he pushed open the door, stuck out a leg, and extended a hand with a twenty in it toward the driver. Aldo accepted it with a familiar nod of thanks for a thirteen-dollar tip on a seven-dollar fare.

Hopping out, he awkwardly slid between two tightly parked cars and weaved between the masses of people, quickly reaching the stainless steel handle of a weathered glass door of a small, discreet diner in the center of the financial district. Pushing it open and passing through, he turned off the chaotic noise of the street and welcomed the low hum of the dining area.

The room was full, jammed actually, as all the regulars assumed their favorite tables. Sal's was along the wall, so he could see everyone around him, underneath a yellowing wall of pictures from acquaintances from the years past. There were no movie stars or politicians, just the people in the neighborhood who owned it and made things happen.

At this time of day, Sal could always be found there. No reserved signs were needed, as everyone had their own space, and out of respect, allowed him his. Looking around the room through the muffled fluorescent lights, he mentally took attendance of those present, and most importantly those that weren't. The diner was small, with the lunch counter running along the length of the right side of the room. Behind it ran the waitresses with shimmering displays of pies, cakes, and cannoli in a glass showcase. It was made of brilliant aluminum with a tilted mirror at the top of each shelf reflecting an aerial snapshot of each choice.

The rest of the diner was a dull yellow, formally a brilliant gold that had grown tired and had begun to succumb to the grease and the grey of years of cigar smoke. The large picture window at the front allowed for some sense of space, and with a crowded sidewalk of people pushing by, patrons felt grateful to be in the diner and not out there.

"Sal!" came an urgent call from the direction of the counter. A portly, bald man in a blue dress shirt and black pants forced his way past the cash register, briefly pinning the young girl who was making change against the open drawer, her face grimacing slightly at the squeezing of her kidneys, followed by a disgusted stare at the owner of the meaty fingers that seemed to linger on her butt.

"Sal!" he blurted out again, obviously overjoyed at his arrival. Holding out his arms, he was embraced as a long-lost relative with a deep, meaningful hug.

"Jeez, Louie, I come here every Wednesday morning, and you act like you haven't seen me in years!"

"I tell you, Sal," and Louie, looking at him as if giving him directions to the only bridge in the city that was open, "someone leaves one day, and you may never see them again. I'm always glad to see my friends again."

Two palms suddenly engulfed Sal's face as if he had dove headfirst into a large fleshy pillow.

"Okay, okay, okay," Sal responded as the palm hug parted. Reaching into his left pocket, he pulled out the handkerchief he had folded and placed it firmly into Louie's hand, closing the fingers tightly around it with the other hand.

Pointing sharply at Louie's chest, he spoke slowly and softly. "Here's what I promised." With a warm smile, Louie nodded. Taking the handkerchief, he awkwardly reached around his girth and slipped into his back pocket.

"Is he here?" Sal asked.

"Yeah, he got here a few minutes ago. He's in the back," he said, referring to a small room off of the main diner, which was open but empty with the exception of one man. The large opening could be partitioned off if needed, the vinyl accordion screen pushed awkwardly to the side. Only the truly connected were allowed a seat in this small den.

The single gentleman who sat there was of medium build and wore a dark blue shirt, open at the neck, with a grey sport coat hanging loosely over his shoulders. His hair was thick, the sign of a young man, yet the edges were beginning to recede from stress. He was talking on a cell phone in a hushed voice, occasionally stroking his hair back, leaning his palm on his cheek, nodding at the information he was receiving.

"He's by himself. Good," Sal said more as an affirmation than a fact. "Ready, Louie?"

"It's taken care of," Louie said with a weak smile. Then he turned and pushed his way back behind the woman at the register and into the tight space behind the counter.

Sal navigated through the standing customers and around the tightly placed tables. Reaching the space separating the open room and the noisy diner, Sal hesitated. At first, the young man was engrossed in his conversation, but as if sensing Sal's presence, he suddenly looked up and motioned for Sal to come over with a stern look and a snap of the fingers.

Sal walked over quietly, sliding into the empty red vinyl seat of the booth across from the gentleman and waited quietly, his arms folded on the table in front of him.

"Okay . . . okay . . . okay, just a second," he said into the cell phone. Placing the open receiver against his shoulder, he looked directly at Sal with the cold stare of an interrogator.

"How do you get blood out of stucco?" he asked.

Sal hesitated. "Inside or outside?"

"Inside."

"White paint?"

"Just a second." He turned back to the phone. "The room's got white paint, right?" Of course, on the walls." He shook his head at the waste of time this was becoming.

He turned the phone back to his shoulder. "Yeah, it's white." He waited for Sal's reply with a look that said the conversation was over except for the good-bye.

"Bleach and a wire brush at first. When it's dry, sponge paint the stain. It'll totally disappear. The stain will never come through."

The gentleman repeated what Sal had said, followed by another "okay," and then a sharp snap as the phone closed.

"Dumb shits," he said. "I told 'em, if you're going to tune up a customer, take him to the Forest Preserve. Nobody can hear you, and who cares if there's blood on the leaves. If someone finds it, they'll think it's Bambi or something. Jesus." He ran his hand roughly through his hair and fell back into the seat in a slouch.

Sitting across from him, Sal waited patiently as his boss cooled down. Sal eyed him cautiously. Antonio "The Bull" Signardo was known for his quick, violent temper and sudden rush to action before all the information was in. For that reason, his life had always been expected to be short, but his rise in the crew had been meteoric and brutal. His luck, however, had held up, and the cards always played into his hands. With the sudden death of his uncle, Frankie "The Pipe" Vichusi, in prison, Antonio assumed the reins as the self-appointed capo by climbing the normal rungs of the ladder—fear, cunning, and paranoia. At just barely thirty-two, Antonio had it all—money, position, and a hunger for more.

Taking a deep, cleansing breath, Antonio stared hard at Sal. "Saleeeee," he began.

Sal exhaled—the first sign of a calm conversation.

"Your crew did well last week. Two hijacks and a very important collection."

Sal smiled softly, hunched his shoulders slightly. "Just doin' my job."

"And a good job it was. Now with Mr. Abe's up-front money covered, we can just keep hitting him for the interest."

Antonio leaned forward, placed his elbows on the table, and dropped his voice to a whisper. "This week . . ." He hesitated, moving the salt shaker closer to the menu in the wire holder so it was symmetrical with the pepper. "I want you to start to move into the near west-side docks across the bay."

Sal was stunned. The docks had been divided up years ago and had stayed that way for generations. The turf wars had to stop because the fighting among the families was killing the business. "The Pipe" had fought in those wars, earning his name by the weapon he chose. It was only after a truce forged by the four families, dividing the bay up equally, that could they make the docks profitable. Moving in on one family's territory would break the truce, and it would start all over again. He winced at the thought of losing any of the men he had cultivated over the last few years. The constant moving and stakeouts. Cleaning brains out of his trunk again.

"With due respect," Sal began quietly, "the truce has been very profitable for us." He tried to smile as he talked, but he could see the darkness forming behind "The Bull's" eyes. "Perhaps, not at this time," he added, hoping to show deferment and not denial at the suggestion.

"Look, Sal," he began. "You've been a rock in this family for years. I worked on your crew for a few of those years, remember?"

Sal nodded.

"So I have a lot of respect for you, but I'm the big dog now. I'm calling the shots, and if I see an opportunity that will benefit all of us, I'm going to take it."

"But it has been awfully good for a really long time. I mean, 'The Pipe' always said—"

"Fuck 'The Pipe'!" Antonio growled. "He grew soft in his old age. He could've had it all, but he blinked. Lost the edge. I won't make the same mistake. Besides, I'm sure they're planning the same thing against us. Push us out. Push us back to doing parking meters and vending machines again. Trust me," he pointed at Sal's chest as if to press the point into his soul, "they are thinking the same thing."

"Still, 'The Pipe' always said—"

"Didn't you just hear what I said?" Antonio's eyes grew dark, and his jaw set.

At this point, Louie entered the room and stewarded two cups of coffee to them. Sal looked at Louie, smiling faintly in gratitude, and then looked back at Antonio with intent.

Sensing the tension, Louie softly patted Sal on the shoulder and disappeared behind the booth through the swinging kitchen door. Alone again, Antonio had taken the pause to rethink, but his edge remained. With a bear paw of a hand, he scooped up the cup and took a large swig. Returning it, he winced slightly at a bitter aftertaste.

"You old timers don't understand, do you?" he began. Leaning forward, he seemed to suddenly tower over Sal. "The world has changed. It belongs to guys like me." He tapped himself on the chest with two fingers. "I take. I'm the taker, because if I don't do it, someone will. And that other someone, he may not be so generous to guys like you."

He reached over the cup with another swipe, another gulp, and a return to the saucer, only now his hand lingered, holding onto the cup. "All I ask is that you show me the respect of a boss. Show me the respect that you showed 'The Pipe.' The respect that I have now earned and deserve."

Slowly, the edge seemed to fade a little. The eyes softened, and the jaw relaxed.

Sal began again. "'The Pipe' earned our respect. He made the truce to keep us alive."

"To hell with him!" Antonio said in a sudden burst of energy. "He was soft, and he was weak, and he was past his time! He needed to be pushed aside!" And there was a pause as Antonio's pride and selfishness welled up, and a slim, sharp fact slipped out of his shriveling thought process and burst out of his mouth. "That's why I had him whacked."

This statement lay between them, and Sal looked down at the table as if it were a platter, and on it was a large heaving fish, gulping for air as it died.

"You killed 'The Pipe'?" he asked softly.

Antonio nodded sharply.

"You killed your own uncle. Your own flesh and blood?"

"Fuck ya!" Antonio said and then took another swig of his coffee. Sal glanced at the cup before Antonio's hand slipped away, and he noticed the scarred knuckles from ancient fights, the cuts from teeth and glass, a bite mark from a long-ago dispensed-with bookie and neatly trimmed fingernails beginning to assume a bluish tint.

"I ordered it, and that's a fact," Antonio said.

"Actually," Sal began. "It's a confession. You see, I went to my PO box a few days ago, and in there were the usual bills and flyers and other crap." He reached into his chest pocket and pulled out a folded letter, yellowed on the margins from extreme heat, yet the ink was dark and the print clear. "And here was this letter." Sal shrugged. "Don't know how it got there; it's over three years old according to the postmark." He laid it on the table. "It's from 'The Pipe', and it's dated three months before he died. Three months before he was beaten to death with pipes in prison."

Antonio laughed. "I thought that would be a nice touch, 'The Pipe' getting the pipe." As he talked, a thin line of drool began to leave the corner of his mouth. He clumsily wiped it away with the back of his hand. Suddenly feeling a chill, he shifted awkwardly and began flexing his fists and moving his fingers.

"What's truly interesting is that in the letter, 'The Pipe' tells me everything about what you are going to do, and that you are trying to kill him and that we are to take care of you first before you take care of him."

The silence returned. Where there was once a strong vocal force sitting across from Sal, there now was only a fading form slowly sinking into the seat.

"You talk about respect," Sal said. "I gave you my respect despite my own assumptions. My respect now lays with my former boss, the man who protected me. The man who earned my respect through his deeds and not just his words. I will give him my utmost respect by fulfilling his last wish."

Antonio blinked hard. It was beginning to register that something was horribly wrong. The desire for self-preservation suddenly appeared with the impulse to get up and run, but the wires that connected his brain to his legs and arms had been severed. Bobbing his head down, he stared at his numb and useless appendages. Helplessly, a long stream of drool spilt over his lip and puddled on his thigh.

Unable to speak, his head bobbed up loosely. Blinking hard, he was able to see Sal again, but behind him, leaning into the booth there were now three shapes. The center one was Louie, with a tight bundle of garbage bags in his hand. The lines in his face were set deep, and his eyes were cold and unfocused, a hangman's stare. The shapes on either side of him were much larger, and in their hands he could glimpse the shine of a cleaver blade in the one and a baseball bat in the other.

"Aitor!" he blurted out at Sal through numbed lips.

Sal smiled. "It's not about me. It's about all of us." He paused as he rose to get out of the seat. "And about respect."

Straightening his jacket, he turned away from the booth and walked over to the vinyl accordion curtain that was hanging loosely against the wall. With a snap, he slowly moved it across the entrance until it had sealed the small dining area off from the main room, feeling secure to be on the outside. Pushing the magnet on the curtain handle against the magnet on the facing wall, he secured the curtain and turned away to walk through the busy main room, waving to Bruno "Three chins" Antonelli seated at his regular table, and patting Vincent "The Mask" Bruceni firmly on the shoulders while he ate his lunch. Approaching his usual small table in the corner, he faced the room beneath an aged picture of a grinning "Pipe" shaking the hand of a much younger Sal.

Emma's letter

—•—

It was unusually warm for March. The tall mounds of snow that dotted curbs and corners were fading away, leaving greasy spots in the gutters. Rivulets of melted snow trickled across the parking lot and disappeared into fresh cracks in the asphalt, as the hardened ice capsules from a month of snow storms, began to slowly fade.

Emma wanted to take advantage of the clear weather to be outside on the porch. Rising out of her living room chair, she cautiously balanced herself on her frail legs as she rolled the walker in front of her toward the front door. Having achieved that, she paced herself, taking two steps and then a step with the walker until she reached the front door. She paused to gaze longingly up the stairway leading to the darkened second floor. It had been three years since she last visited, and she hoped to again. Reaching the front door, she successfully opened it and then used her walker to brace open the screen door to the porch as she navigated the narrow doorway. Getting through the door was always treacherous. Nearly catching her white sweater on the spring, she leaned slightly to the left, and the loop slipped off the metal.

With determination, she now continued her trek to the long, white porch swing.

Reaching the swing, she took the plaid blanket that she had draped over her walker handles and half placed, half tossed it across the seat. She then, with small deliberate steps, turned herself until the back of her knees struck the wood of the seat. Letting gravity finally have its way, she leaned back and fell onto the seat, causing the wood to groan from the force and the chain to snap to attention, waking from a winter of dormancy.

She let the momentum swing the seat until she felt the energy begin to fade. Pulling the white, woolen sweater tighter across her chest, she reached for the pole on the side of the swing that her grandson had constructed. It was secured to the wood of the porch and ran from the floorboards to the porch ceiling, which also supported the swing. It was thin, not designed for support, but rather for a handle where Emma could grasp it and use it to swing the chair without using her knotted legs or crippled back for support.

Grasping it tightly with a ruined hand, knuckles knotted from decades of housework and shifting beer bottles at the brewery, she maintained the momentum of the swing as it creaked back and forth on a beautiful day in her seventy-fourth spring.

Many of the usual suspects were out this afternoon. The postman was making his rounds at the far end of the block while the "Handie Car" from the neighborhood grocer was making its deliveries. Mrs. Roach was out walking her golden retriever across the way. It already had its coat, cut into a summer style, and it pulled at the lead as it tried to get to all the new odors. Some of the children were already home from school, and she could hear their squeals and yells from a handful of backyards as they stretched their lungs with the outside air.

A gentle breeze suddenly pushed through the porch, bringing a sudden warmth, a harbinger of things to come. She closed her eyes and tried to breathe it in to her shallow lungs as far as she could. The years of smoking prevented the depth, but the flavor was all she needed; it brought memories of past springs and the promise of more.

When she opened her eyes, her daughter had just pulled up in front of the house and was beginning to exit her sedan. Emma immediately picked up a feeling of heaviness, a weight her daughter, Anna, seemed to be carrying that had to be shared. At fifty-four, her daughter was the perfect reflection of her father, gone twelve years now. She had his narrow, clear blue eyes, which would never lie to her.

Anna flashed a forced smile and quick wave, yet looked down at the sidewalk as she crossed over the curb and walked up to the porch. With deliberately measured steps, she trod up the stairs leading to the porch, her hands deep in her jacket pockets, shoulders almost hunched over.

"Hi, Mom."

"Looks like you lost your best friend." Emma took a measure of her daughter as she slumped down in the swing next to her. "Who died?" she asked, looking away just as two little girls ran into the front yard in hot pursuit of a small, yellow cat.

Anna wanted to protest, but she had played this game too many times to resist. First there was the rebuttal, the pensive attitude, and then the accusation of pessimism sometimes followed finally by the acquiescence of fact. The fact was the most difficult, sometimes taking an event just short of an act of God.

"It's Delia, Mom."

Emma nodded.

"It was very sudden, Mom," Anna continued, hoping some of the early facts would loosen the cold façade. "She apparently was cooking breakfast when she had a heart attack, right there at the stove. The neighbor saw the smoke and was able to get the fire out before the whole house went up, but there was nothing they could do for her."

Emma nodded again. "Not the way I would have chosen."

"For yourself, Mom?"

"For her." Emma's steely glance cut into Anna. "You know the history."

Anna was sullen. She had hoped the finality would soften her mother's resolve. But she always underestimated her fortitude. Respect was always the expectation, and slights were seldom forgiven.

"You know about the wedding. The time I gave to her daughter when she was young, and Delia was running around. The effort it took to keep everything together for them despite my own hardships." Emma spoke in curt, sharp sentences as if instructing a driving school student during an exam.

Ana knew the script. A lifetime of giving and no reward at the end. A commitment that was extended and yet never acknowledged.

"It was all the fault of that . . ." and here the word would stick. A letter would form with the pursing of the lips, yet the brain—in an act of decency—failed to give it the air it needed to be launched like an angry hornet. Relaxing slightly, she supplied the only word that she could use safely. "Selfish."

"Please, Mom," Anna said, closing her eyes tightly, trying to mentally work through the minefield she was entering. Trying to negotiate a sense of compassion and reason from a shrew that only knows black and white, dark and light, obligation versus desire. "I don't think it was intentional. You know how confusing weddings are to begin with," she fumbled a little with the words. "There's . . . there's . . . there are calls to make and plans to decide on and . . . and . . ."

"Invitations to mail," Emma finished for her. "And if you know the important people to invite, those are easy—unless you're simply a . . ." The word formed again. It was there on the cusp, the edge of existence, requiring only a puff of wind to exist, to be a force of description, sharp as a knife and hard as a bullet. But once again, the nymphs of decent thought redirected the wind to a distant orifice where the sound was subtle yet distinct in its arrival. "Delia knew I was forgotten."

"Mother, you're getting worked up."

"No I'm not; this is not worked up," she said in measured tones.

"Yes it is. Trust me; there are signs." Anna leaned away from her mother slightly and then stood up. She half leaned, half sat against the white porch railing across from her mother. Her hands were placed together in her lap, as if hoping for some guidance from another source. Across the street, the girls had dashed behind some larger junipers, giggling at the prospect of capturing the cat, unaware that the feline had slipped out the other end and was casually staring at their futility from the front yard.

"Mother," Anna began softly, "you cannot hold these grudges against someone for something they did long ago." Leaning forward to press her point, she said, "Intentional or not."

121

"I raised you to have the manners of a lady and to have respect toward others. Anything short of that in return is the sign of a lesser person." And then the drop in tone, the glare over the wire framed bifocals and the tightened shoulders. "It's not Christian."

"Don't do that, Mother."

"Do what?" Emma replied innocently.

"Quote the Bible."

"I didn't quote any such thing," Emma said innocently, as if being mistakenly accused of walking out of a store with a scarf she hadn't paid for.

"And don't use the tone either. I know how hard you truly are!"

With a convenient tremble in her hands and the apologetic stare of a cherub, Emma sat there for a few seconds, her mouth slightly open, her eyes fixed on her daughter's face like an assassin scoping through the sight before the trigger is pulled.

"You've chosen Delia over me. That's it, isn't it?"

"That's not true, Mom, and you know it." Anna breathed in frustration, hurt at getting attacked for being the messenger.

"You always took her side; you always did special favors for her; you always wanted to be with that . . ."

And the word was there again. Swollen in the upper lip, set in the lower jaw, prepared to tumble over. But there it rested, to go no further.

"I was trying to help her, Mom. Just trying to be a good Christian."

With hands thin and knotted from arthritis, and raised veins like blue cables running down her forearms and wrists, Emma rose in a slow effort. As the walker creaked from her weight, she began the shuffle back into the house from the porch.

"Don't talk to me about being Christian," She said softly in her slow shuffle past her daughter toward the screen door. "You will be judged, dear, and as your mother, I will pray for you."

Anna looked away, shaking her head. She watched the yellow cat now licking its paws in the spring grass in the center of the front yard. It was lying down, having lost interest in the girls. As the girls searched in vain, their voices rising in frustration as they bellowed the cat's name, it raised a paw to knock away a moth. Engrossing herself in the moment and trying to somehow get her arms around her mother's attitude, Anna failed to hear the screen door shut as Emma went into the house, the school bell ring from down the block, the mother calling for the children to come in to lunch, and the postman walking up and setting a long, white envelope on the steps while sifting through the other letters of the day.

Nathan's letter

—•—

"No, no, no!" Nathan exclaimed, forcefully placing himself between the cook and the table. Cautiously, yet with intent, he reached over to the young cook's right hand, slipped two fingers over the handle of the knife that was being held loosely in the man's palm, and confronted a tomato rolling forlornly in front of him.

"Okay," Nathan exhaled, exasperated. "Here is the knife you have sharpened, and unfortunately all of our knives." He pressed on the tomato with the tip of the knife, and the skin dented a little before it gave in and a quarter-inch thick slide flopped away from the main vegetable, its red pulp and yellow seeds spilling out onto the cutting board.

"Did you see it?" he asked, almost spitting into the face of the small Hispanic man standing a half step beside him. "The skin dented a little before the cut, and the slice flopped away."

Reaching for a clean knife within easy reach, he gripped the handle with the familiarity of an old friend. "Now this is the knife I have sharpened."

Seemingly without even touching the tomato, Nathan pushed it through and displayed a clean slice of tomato pasted to the side of the blade, seeds and pulp obediently in place.

"As you saw, there was no indenture from the blade, therefore no bruising of the skin, and the tomato is cut cleanly." He held the knife—tomato attached—up as a display. "This tomato does not even know it has been sliced."

He laid the knife down on the board.

"These knives must . . . be . . . sharp," he said, closing his eyes to try to ward off the headache rising in the back of his mind like a humid August sunrise, searing and bright, but not yet hot. "If you cannot keep them sharp, then I have no use for you, and you are gone." He squinted down at the thin man, barely twenty years old, with his hands held uncomfortably behind him, trying to contemplate how he could lose a job he had for only two days.

"Do you understand, Jorge?"

Jorge gave a quick nod of understanding and then rubbed his nose with the back of his hand, pushing against the thin black moustache he had been trying to grow for the last six months.

"Good, now go wash your hands." Nathan turned away with the disgust. He walked out of the kitchen and toward the back door, where Alexi, the sous chef, was checking in the weekly shipment of fish off of a paneled delivery truck in the alley.

Slipping past Alexi and the stacked crates of ice and fish lined up against the brick wall, he blinked at the sudden brightness of the summer afternoon sun.

"Got a headache?" Alexi asked as he checked off the fish versus the manifest.

"No," Nathan lied.

"Want one?"

Nathan shrugged as he took a pack of cigarettes out of his front pocket, tapped out a fresh one, and slipped it into his lips. "No."

"Well here it is. No orange roughy today, didn't make the plane."

With a cupped hand, Nathan lit the end and pulled a deep breath. Closing his eyes, he could feel the waves of pain beginning to gather, a hum of activity purring in his ears.

"If I remember right, wasn't that the special for tonight?" Nathan ventured.

"Yep."

"So now we have to come up with an award-winning dinner that must be reasonably priced with something we don't even know we have enough of."

"Yep."

"And we have to do it in three and a half hours, which is when we put the first ordered plate on the table."

"Yes, sir." With a flare, Alexi signed the manifest. He motioned with one hand to the driver to get his paperwork, while nodding to Jose, an orderly standing by the side of the truck, ready to move the food into the cooler.

Finding a small stack of fish just about crotch high, Nathan turned and sat down as he exhaled slowly, rubbing the bridge of his nose.

"Don't sit on the fish," Alexi said as he took his copy of the paperwork and headed back into the restaurant.

"Haddock soothes my ass," Nathan replied, followed by a whispered, "Fuck."

"Is Tony in yet?" he barked at the vacant doorway.

"No," came the response through the closing metal door.

Trying to think, he rubbed his brow and flipped through the rolodex of recipes in his head. Nothing came to mind with what he had just ordered or had in the cooler.

Deciding that sitting on iced fish while in the hot sun was making his headache worse, he stood, stomped out the half-smoked cigarette, and began to rub the back of his right hand with his left thumb. Glancing down, he saw the dark blue moon tattoo with three evenly spaced stars over it that he had had inked at eighteen when he was in the navy.

He always felt this ritual would give him luck when he was a young man. Having used up all his luck surviving the navy, he did it now as more of a habit than as a ritual. As he walked back into the kitchen, his knee scrapped against the corner of one of the fish crates.

"Will someone put this shit away?" he bellowed as two stewards came racing out of the cooler and through the metal door, having already moved half of it.

Without turning around, he walked through the gleaming metal kitchen, somewhat empty, but far from silent as the cooking staff and stewards were beginning to trickle in for the evening shift. As he walked past the burners, shelves, and burgeoning cooler doors, he could hear the even, steady scraping sound as a suddenly nervous Jorge diligently worked the edges of the knives on the rat tail. In hope of giving the boy confidence, Nathan gripped the cook's shoulder firmly as he passed by.

"Reuben, tell Marsha to change the menu to Halibut Provencale!" he yelled through the curtain to an empty dining area.

His destination was the small office just off the kitchen—a large closet with just enough room for a desk and a small couch. Walking in, he sat down in the middle of the couch, facing an empty but surprisingly organized desk. Slapping his forearms together, he slipped them down between his legs and stared at the fading watercolor paintings scattered unevenly across the walls. These were done by Tony's wife, and they reflected his love and admiration for her far above her ability to paint. In his head, the waves were beginning to slap against rocks a little harder, and the seas were becoming a little rougher. In addition to the pain, he knew the migraine would begin to compromise his attitude, and he prayed that he could keep it together through as least the first few sittings.

Anthony Carrasco strolled into the office about ten minutes later. Tucked under his left arm was a tied accordion file, and in his right was a small coffee. Anthony was short in stature with the rounded, thick shape of a man who has loved food all his life. He was wearing a light brown sport coat over a white golf shirt, and he looked fresh, like a man newly born. Glancing at Nathan forlornly perched on the sofa, he studied him briefly before sliding behind his desk. "My head chef is in my office before 2:00. This is not a good sign, he remarked as he placed the accordion file in a wire basket. As he set the cup down, a bright gold ID bracelet slipped down to his wrist, followed by a solid gold bracelet dangling a discreet but noticeable half moon.

When Nathan had first interviewed for the job three years ago, Tony had noticed his tattoo and then revealed the moon to him to show that theirs was a kinship, a fate. Tony offered him the job on the spot, and it had worked out well ever since.

"We got fucked on the fish again," Nathan said sullenly to the jaundiced floor tile under his feet.

Anthony pursed his lips. "Is this an invoicing problem?" he asked softly.

"No."

A silence.

"How about a failing cooler, theft, or marketing issue?"

Nathan slowly motioned no, his thinning hair beginning to shine with sweat.

"Could this be . . . ," Anthony shrugged with fake obliviousness, "perhaps . . . a menu problem?"

Nathan slowly nodded his head in agreement.

Anthony took a sip of his coffee as he enjoyed the control he now had over his chef's arrogance.

"My dear friend, if there were any of the problems I mentioned earlier, I could help, but menus I do not do."

Nathan raised his head and leaned back into the couch. Anthony readily noticed the reddening of the ears, the sweating, and glazing of the eyes. He had known Nathan long enough to know that a tempest in his skull was brewing and would turn all of the issues into a pulsing morass. This had to be resolved quickly before it edged into a tantrum.

"However, I am in a good mood today. Let me make a call," Anthony said. Taking a gleaming sliver phone from his jacket pocket, he pushed one dial and was almost instantly rewarded with a response.

"Bruno!" Anthony exclaimed, having connected with the chef of one of his three other restaurants in the city. "Hey, got a question! That new orange roughy recipe you tried, how did it go over?" Being a managing owner required him to visit all of his restaurants daily either personally or through an assigned proxy to evaluate. He knew the answer to the question, yet needed his regular kowtow from this chef on an experiment that failed miserably, leaving twenty pounds of rapidly aging fish in a cooler six miles away.

"Uh," Anthony followed, "so what are you going to do with the product?" Anthony followed with a few distressed grunts. "Well, before you do that, let me suggest this. Bring the product over to Nathan's place. We'll see if we can move it tonight, and then it's out of your sight and off of your books. Okay?" Anthony nodded softly as he gazed up at the walls at a yellowy water color of a black stick figure with engorged hands on a retriever-shaped donkey.

"Good, get over here as fast as you can, and I will let you know how much Nathan appreciates this favor when I stop over tonight, okay?" Anthony nodded hard and replied with "Good!" before snapping the phone shut.

Anthony leaned back in his leather chair, regaling in his role as negotiator. "Does this solve the problem? Yes it does." Anthony answered himself very quickly.

Nathan said softly, "We already made the menu out for halibut."

"Marsha!" Anthony screamed. Not getting a response within a nanosecond of bellowing, another "Marsha!" emerged.

Anthony smiled at Nathan as the quick shuffling of wooden heels on tile floor alerted him of her approach.

A thin-faced woman in her early twenties peered around the corner, her brilliant Irish red hair changing the tint in the room. A long silver earring with a small bat on the end swung across her freckled cheek.

Somewhat taken aback, Anthony stared at the ornament.

"It's July," he blurted out.

"So?" she replied.

"What's with the fucking bat?"

"I like fucking bats. I have one with two bats fucking. Would you like to see that tomorrow? What do you want? I'm busy."

"No to the first question, and did we run the menu cards for tonight?"

"I was just getting ready to—why?"

"There's a change."

Exhaling, she dropped her shoulder, and her thin, tall frame seemed to slink into the doorway. "Jesus, now what?"

Anthony held up a thick palm in an effort to calm the rhetoric and cool the attitude.

"All you have to do is take off the Halibut and add . . ." He turned toward Nathan as a gesture to complete the thought.

Nathan blinked a few times and then methodically added, "Orange roughy . . . in a sherry reduction sauce . . . over garlic rice . . . and steamed summer vegetables."

"Got it?" Anthony asked with overt politeness.

"Got it," she replied with disgust and stormed away.

"What is this favor going to cost me?" Nathan asked, a little wide-eyed.

Anthony took another sip from his coffee, leaned back over his desk, laced his fingers together on the stained calendar from two years ago, and smacked his lips. "Well," he began, I need a chef to present a brunch for a number of . . . ," he thought very carefully on this, "legislators in two weeks. You just volunteered."

"I don't do brunches," Nathan offered in a weak defense.

"Well, Bruno doesn't know it yet, but his failed recipe adventure now requires him to present a buffet for my daughter's thirteenth birthday party. If you wish to switch, I'm sure he would be very agreeable."

Nathan didn't hesitate. "Will salmon be okay?"

Anthony chuckled slightly. "As I said earlier, I don't do menu problems."

The loud sound of dragging heels announced the return of Marsha.

"Oh, by the way, Mister Personality," she said in Nathan's direction, "There is an envelope for you by the bar. Please attend to it." She flashed a quick, fake smile and then disappeared around the corner, the sound of her dragging heels blending in with the crash of pans and thud of pots and the crew began to gear up the kitchen for the night's performance.

Nathan arose, the final details of the dinner slipping into place in his mind like pegs and holes, and he exited the room, not noticing the casual affirmation of Anthony with a raised coffee cup as recognition. As he entered the kitchen, the station chefs casually grouped around him, wringing hands on aprons, fists on hips, brows knitted with intent as Nathan quickly dispatched the duties, sequencing times and ingredients.

Having received their orders, each hustled to their stations, and the machine that was the kitchen began to ramp up in activity and purpose. As the others split from the group and attended their stations, Nathan kept his sous chef and instructed him that he would not/could not stay. He was hoping that he would last to the third seating, but the ringing in his head began to pitch higher, and his concentration was getting difficult to hold. As first mate, he could receive the ship at any time.

Walking to the front through the thick, black curtains leading into the dining area, he was greeted by a ten-degree drop in temperature and an elaborate, elegant seating arrangement with an old-world French motif. The waitresses hadn't even met to learn their stations; they were still smoking in the alley with the dishwashers and bus boys.

Walking over to the heavy wooden bar at the far corner of the room, he leaned over into the end tall chair and stared at the white postal emblem on the envelope in front of him. Reaching into his front pocket, he pulled out the buck knife he carried, snapped the blade open, and effortlessly slit the end of the package open. Snapping the knife back into place and returning it to his pocket, he turned the package over, allowing a form letter and a small brown envelope to slide out onto the waxed surface of the bar.

The migraine was beginning its first swell, and he was preparing for it mentally, which made it difficult to concentrate on the paper in front of him. He read the apology letter from the postmaster three times before he understood what it said. Crumpling it and tossing it into the garbage can at the entrance to the bar, he slid the envelope in front of him and stared at the words.

The envelope was small and dirty brown, the color of cheap paper and the ages of time. It was addressed to him, or rather the address where he had lived three years ago with his second wife and three sons. His fourth and oldest child from his first wife had graduated college and moved away. He had joined a research group on its way to the deepest jungles of Chile. When he arrived, he wrote to them regularly.

Then he disappeared. In searching for him, all he could ascertain was that he separated from the group a few days to follow a hunch and never arrived at the airport for the flight home. No clues, no trail, no Steven.

Putting the clues together from the envelope, Nathan recognized the national stamp, the processing marks as it left Chile and had entered the United States, and the return address Steven had written, the same as all the letters before. What drew his attention was the postmark date. He gulped hard as he realized that it was postmarked the day before he disappeared. This was Steven's last letter.

Reaching over the bar, he scanned quickly and plucked an open but nearly full bottle of bourbon from the forest of bottlenecks before him.

"Marsha!" he yelled.

She immediately stuck her head out with the agitation of someone who didn't need anyone's attention at that moment. "Yeah?" she bellowed back.

"Tell Arturo the kitchen is his. I'm gone." Clutching the bottle and letter tightly, he stormed out the front door to the roughened black jeep he kept parked in the adjacent lot.

Nathan sat uncomfortably in the lime green, long plastic booth seat of the small diner deep in the city, his former significant other across from him, now in a far less significant position, with the opened letter placed on the table equidistance between them. Zoe had been crying, and the redness of her eyes was accentuated by the heavy black eye liner she wore. They both stared at the letter, the thin black ink of a cheap and fading pen on the brownish paper supplied by a village with no means. "So tell me this again. To make sure I understand everything here," she said, folding her arms partly in defiance, partly from the cool air coming from the ceiling vent on an overcharged air-conditioning system.

"I would not lie to you," Nathan began, interrupted by a sudden sputter of her disbelief, "at least about something this serious. Come on," he pleaded. "This is our son I'm talking about, our firstborn who disappeared somewhere in Chile without any clue, without a sign," he choked a little, "and without a body."

For the tenth time, she looked at the envelope and then at her ex-husband.

"What do you want to do?" she asked quietly.

At that moment, a woman at the next table began a loud conversation on her cell phone. As the tempo of the conversation increased, her volume also rose until Zoe and Nathan were suddenly in the middle of this woman's trouble with her bank.

Setting her jaw, Zoe quietly reached over and tapped the table to get the woman's attention. Turing away from her phone briefly, she saw a middle-aged woman smiling yet glaring directly into her eyes.

"Sweetheart," she began softly, "if you don't turn your volume down to this level I'm talking at right now, I'm going to take that phone and shove it up your ass so far the antennae is going to come out your belly button, okay?"

Seeing a short, balding man in a blue dress shirt suddenly pass by, the cell phone woman quickly reached out and grabbed his sleeve.

"Are you the manager?" the woman inquired intensely.

The man nodded in agreement.

"That woman just insulted me!" she protested.

"Oh," the man answered. He glanced at Zoe and then hurriedly escaped through the swinging doors leading into the kitchen.

"You see, lady," Zoe continued, "he's the manager, but I'm the fucking owner. I've got shoving rights."

139

Suffering her last insult, the woman snapped her phone shut, gathered her belongings, and stormed out, pushing aside the young waitress coming to take her order.

"Another returning customer," Nathan said.

"Perhaps if you hadn't exercised your shoving rights on the waitresses, we'd still be together," she said, crossing her arms once again.

Nathan's face twisted, and he placed his hands flat on the table. "You always come back to that. It's always about what I did or didn't do that you want to fight over again and again."

"It's not what you did, it's who you did!" Zoe began to press forward, hot emotions began to bubble up, and suddenly Nathan was back where he was four years ago when the infidelity was first discovered.

Nathan stopped, his hands still flat on the table, his breathing rapid but regular. "Look, I came here to give you the clues I had on where our son is, not to fight old wars. You got the diner, I got my life back. That's fair to me, and I'm okay with that."

She was ready to react, but the evenness of his tone and the dead stare of his eyes left her in a détente, and the reasoning returned. She dropped her guard and raised her arms once more. "What do you want to do?" she asked a second time.

"I'm going to Chile to find him. The letter is very specific on what village he is leaving from, what pass into the mountains he is taking, and what he's looking for. I'm going to start there."

Nathan exhaled and leaned back into the booth, the springs creaking loudly from the shift in balance. "I can get $2,800 now, and I will need another $3,000. Maybe more depending on how long I stay. Can you do it?" he asked.

"I'm in," she replied, nodding.

"I will pay you back within the next few months; the wedding season is coming up and—"

"Just bring our son back." She stopped the tears beginning to well up, and a small drip began to run down her cheek. "Find him," she corrected herself, and for the first time in years, she reached out and placed her hand on top of Nathan's. Lovers long ago vanquished were parents once again.

Stepping off the plane in Arica, Chile, he felt the full thrust of humidity trying to push him back into the plane, like a helpful hand trying to protect him from danger by keeping him away from a bad situation. The smells were an odd mix of rot from decaying vegetation, to sweet from the flowering foliage. Mixed among this was the harsh aroma of humankind, the brutish pungency of diesel and jet fuel, and an agrarian cloud of goats and llama.

Struggling to walk down the ramp with a woman with three children in front of him and a pushy businessman behind him, who was trying to filter the third-world stench through a white handkerchief, he was able to finally reach the tarmac. Racing into the terminal, the comfort he had hoped for was fleeting. With no central coding systems, the area was wide open and un-informing. There were only red clay walls with a tin roof, the only authority being a few bored guards checking flashing passports, basing their security theories on the fact that if you could get on the plane and fly safely to this destination, there was no need for any further hassle.

Reaching the front of the airport, he easily got a cab, which took him to the only European hotel on the coast and the relief of air-conditioning. Settling into the tiny room in the farthest corner of the hotel, he slipped his duffle bag off his shoulder and onto the floor. He flipped the small suitcase he had onto the bed, which bounced on the rolling mattress and rocked back and forth twice before settling.

After spending a few moments catching his breath, he parted the drapes by the window and gazed out at the grey hub of a city. Tapping his front pocket, he felt the crinkle of paper from the letter. It was already becoming frayed on the edges, and the folds were progressing from cresses to perforations. He ached to read it again, but the fear of it completely falling apart in his hands prevented him. Like a wolf on the edge of the flock, he could feel the migraine beginning again. Luckily there was nowhere to go for the rest of the day, and he anticipated its arrival while glaring out at the gray human condition.

Nathan wondered what would ever bring his son to such a hopeless place. Steven was studying to be an archeologist. His specialty was mummies, and the upper regions of Chile had rich collections of specimens left as sacrifices in the cracks and crevices of the upper Andes. He had been there almost four months, writing regularly, but getting frustrated at finding so little. The last correspondence they had was a quick postcard from a photo shop saying he was on his way home, and after two stopovers in Colombia and Panama, he would be in Chicago within a few days' time. That was four years ago, and it was the last correspondence they ever had from him.

Asking the national authorities to search for him proved futile. "Young people disappear all the time." they said. Besides, he could be anywhere in Central America. According to the manifest, he was never on the return plane home. According to the authorities, he was never in the country.

Without leads and limited funds, there was nowhere to turn. As time went on, the burden crushed the marriage, and the trust and respect shattered like glass falling from a window. With Steven the only child they had together, it was easy to dismiss the marriage as a convenience neither wished for. It was easier to concentrate on the business at hand and be buried in those details rather than go home and face a situation where neither wanted to discuss who was missing at the dinner table. Lack of intent led to lack of desire, and the distractions around, him in particular, made it simpler to walk away. He did try again, with more success, but Steven's loss created a hole in her life that nothing could fill.

His new family seemed to help with the healing. Without them as a distraction, he returned to constantly thinking about Steve, because despite whatever situation he was in, there was always the wondering, the thin amount of clues. He kept asking, *What was Steven feeling when he left? Where did he go? Where is he now?* The images became obsessive, and the farther he tried to put them out of his mind, the harder they fought to return. Then the migraines began.

He slept a restless night in the hotel and then headed down to the main lobby with his duffel bag to check out and get a quick meal of fruit for breakfast from a small store located in the hotel by the main entrance. Finding a small place away from the constant flow of foot traffic, he slid his duffel down and leaned against one of the main pillars in the lobby. He pulled out a map of the area to study where he was to start to look, and with a deep breath, he tried to formulate a plan.

In Steven's new letter, he had mentioned the Minimi River and a village called Itaci as the starting point for his journey. Finding a village on the map was easy, but trying to get someone to get him there proved much more difficult. The counterman at the hotel proved to be absolutely useless, refusing to connect him to anyone capable of getting him there and arguing with him about whether the village even existed. Efforts with the other employees proved equally futile. Even the manager refused to discuss it with him, stating that he was currently absorbed by a problem on the roof and could not work on this problem at this time. If he set an appointment for later in the week, the manager would try to make the effort.

Frustrated, he walked out to the front of the hotel. The cab line was busy, and the constant flux of people added to the oppression of the humidity. By late morning, the air was already beginning to become thick and hazy. His aggravation must have been visible because a small, squat man with a pencil-thin moustache and a yellow beret approached him.

"You are to go somewhere?" the man asked in a thick accent, pointing at the map hanging low in Nathan's hand. Nathan glanced at the man; the orange and black flowered shirt matched with loose, brown trousers and open-toed sandals seemed odd. But perhaps it was misleading. After all, it may be a lead.

"Can someone take me here?" Nathan asked, stabbing sharply at the map.

The man stared at the map with a concerned stare. He reached for the map and held it close to his face, his dark brown eyes astutely calculating distance and fee.

"I cannot," he stated sharply. "But I know of someone who can." He looked up at Nathan with the calm assertion of a general with a plan.

"But it will not be cheap. The cost must cover both of the trips . . . to and back, because there is no one there that can drive you to come here."

Nathan knew he was being judged for how much he was worth. He was an American in desperate straits. Surely there was a price to be reached.

"I only have $300. How far will that get me?"

"Not very far I'm afraid. Gasoline is at a premium right now, and with the government stations rationing, we are forced to buy it elsewhere at a much higher price. Five hundred and fifty should be needed I think."

Nathan remembered bartering with the Chileans in the open markets by a restaurant he worked at in a pseudo-apprenticeship. Remembering back to those days, he knew where the margins were. They seemed to be a culture code of value, and he began to work his way toward the middle.

"Five fifty is only possible if I decide not to buy food for the next few days. Three hundred and fifty is possible if I wish to eat."

"Fortunately for you, I know of someone who has a full tank of gas, although the travel will prevent him from getting other paying fares." He shrugged his shoulder in a hard notion. "Perhaps $520?"

Knowing they would squabble to the last dime, Nathan moved in for the deal as any assertive American would.

Wiping away a stream of sweat from his brow with the back of his thumb, he faced the man squarely and slipped his left hand into the front pocket of his khaki shorts.

"This is all I can do. Four hundred dollars now to the driver, for both ways—$200 there, and $200 back. He is to drop me off and return in three days, no more. And this," he pulled his hand out of his pocket to show the corner of a fifty-dollar bill, "is for your troubles."

Sensing the immediacy, the steward's eyes widened at the denomination. Holding his hands up, yet not looking away from the bill, he quoted the hotel line. "I cannot accept any offers of reimbursement as my job is to help the guests." He turned away from Nathan, looked over the line of drivers, and cupped his left hand behind him, as if collecting the rain coming off his beret.

"CanCan!" he barked out as he felt the sharp edge of the bill grace across his palm.

The third driver in the line, a shadow of a man in thick blue pants, a thin, light blue shirt, and a black Nike baseball hat with a worn bill exposing more cardboard than fabric suddenly jumped away from the car door he was leaning on and disappeared behind its wheel.

Within a few moments, he had pulled out of the line and stopped in front of the steward. With a flurry of words, most lost in the background noise behind him, the steward explained the mission at hand, showed him the village and roads on the map, and then seemed to point out the path to the driver, who was nodding in agreement at a frantic pace.

Finally, the driver ducked behind the wheel, and the steward opened the back door, which creaked and popped in resistance.

"Here you are, my friend," he said, handing the map back to Nathan as he slipped into the backseat. "CanCan will take you where you wish to go." Slamming the door shut, he leaned through the window with the grin of a man who had just profited from a deal will done. "Remember, three days." He held up the last three fingers of his right hand, his thumb holding the fifty-dollar bill tightly in his palm. "CanCan will be there and return with or without you." Standing up, he tapped on the roof of the cab, and the taxi limped away from the hotel with the heavy pulse of the stressed engine blending into the noise of the city.

The ancient Ford had a vacuous backseat with a dulled, red plastic seat cushion that was cracked and repaired with packing tape. Creases in the tape were darkened with grime, while the floor was dark brown with a slimy coating of the native soil. As he fitted himself into his seat, he felt the sharpness of the metal springs as they pressed against the thin cushion, the thick stuffing having been worn through years before. Placing his duffel next to him, he heard three sharp *pings* as the seat struggled with the weight, eventually settling to a level even below his own seat.

Staring out of the half-closed window, the aroma of the streets of the village began to drift into the cab. A steady, burnt corn smell laced occasionally with a spike of urine and bovine excrement and old fish began to permeate the cab. Instinctively reaching for the handle, he instead discovered a metal stud where the handle used to be.

"Do you have the handle for the window?" he asked the driver. The young man stared back at him in bewilderment, for much longer than was wise for a vehicle operator, only showing some understanding when Nathan covered his nose and pointed to the worn gear.

Nodding in confirmation, he glanced out the main window, sharply corrected a right-leaning drift to the car, and then disappeared beneath the front passenger side of the cab as he bent over to look, leaving Nathan to stare out of a cracked windshield at peasants along the road, who in turn were staring back at this incredulous self-driving car.

As a sharp left turn came closer, with still no appearance of the driver, Nathan began to quickly judge the three options he had: one, grab the wheel; two, jump from the car and hope for the best; or three, die. In quick review, he concluded that item three may be a follow up to one and two. He leaned forward in his seat and prepared to jump at the wheel. Just as he was gauging his timing, the young man appeared, glanced out the window, made the correction to keep the car on the road, and then tossed a metal object into the backseat.

Landing on the floor with a thick thud, Nathan looked down to see a small pair of greased-stained vice grips slowly being absorbed into the primal soup on the floor. Braving the elements at the expense of preserving his olfactory system, he reached into the slime for the tool, picked it up using as little skin contact as possible, snapped it on the knob, and slowly turned it as the smeared window began its uneven, yet deliberate ascent.

After sometime, he managed to get the window closed, whereupon he discovered most of the smell was actually coming from inside the cab. As the car sped out of the village and onto the thin, narrow road leading into the mountains, he began an even stronger effort to open the window as quickly as he was able to shut it.

His shirt, now stained with sweat from the effort, hung thickly on his shoulders in the humidity, yet the wind, now that they had left the city, was blowing cool air off of the ocean, and he could smell the freshness of a newly broken wave on the rocks along with the subtle smell of salt and fish. It seemed to refresh him, and the paranoia of sudden death began to fade as he grew more comfortable with the bouncing of the cab and the pulse of the engine. Even his duffle bag seemed to enjoy the ride as it bounced appreciably like a small boy on a carnival ride with each pothole the tires struck.

He imagined his son taking the same cab ride on his way to following a hunch or a clue that could lead to a discovery. It could be a false lead, or perhaps a career-making move; the anticipation must have been exciting. Just thinking of the dilemma his son may have been facing made his stomach growl. *Perfect*, he thought, *with my head on a tightrope, it's the perfect time to get an intestinal infection. I hope this poor bastard doesn't drive me there. He may end up driving me to the dock and placing me on a trawler just to get away from me.*

To distract himself, Nathan unzipped his duffle and pulled out an old school backpack of Steven's that he had kept in his closet. He remembered that as he was packing to leave for the airport. He realized at the last minute that he might need a picture of Steven, and with little time before his flight, he grabbed this old school bag of Steven's with a picture ID encased in a plastic tag dangling from a small chain attached to a shoulder strap.

It was worn and tattered from abuse, overstuffing, and neglect. It was the bag his son had used as a senior in high school, and the one Nathan had borrowed as he was hurriedly throwing his possessions into any carryall just to get out of the house during the divorce. Steven was already gone, and his raging soon-to-be ex-wife wasn't initiating a "leave when you're ready" patience but a vocal ultimatum delivered with appropriate volume and necessary urgency. It had been at the bottom of his closet after he had unpacked years ago, and he had long forgotten it, but for some reason, maybe it was because of this relevant, quick-pack-and-go situation, he remembered it.

Now he sat in the back of an infected, antiquated cab and gazed at the photo he cupped with both hands. Some features—eyes, hair, jaw—he recognized as his own, and others—cheekbones, nose, high forehead—were decidedly Zoe's. At seventeen, he could see the man's frame within Steven, outgrowing the boy. Although he had Steven's pictures in a dozen places in his house, many of them of much better quality and design, he suddenly relished this one. It showed a serious look with a playful turn at the end of his smile, tossed hair due to the impromptu moment, but a set to the shoulder that exhibited a powerful sense of confidence. He began to realize how deeply and strongly he missed his son. As the cab wound its way through the passes and toward the small village, Nathan glanced out the window at the harsh peaks of the oncoming mountains. He then returned to the captured face in the tag and rubbed away the tears that had fallen on the scratched plastic case that held his son's picture.

Reaching the edge of a destitute village, the cab rolled to a stop at the first set of houses. Nathan got out, and noticing the air was decidedly cooler, he pulled a jacket out of the duffel and quickly slipped it on. He motioned for the driver to go forward, but the young man returned a blank stare. Nathan tried again, but the driver held up three fingers instead. A little puzzled, Nathan instinctively held up three of his own, curiously looking at them as if the code could be deciphered with his own symbolism. "Three days," the driver blurted out. He then shifted into reverse, completed a perfect three-point turn, and ambled down the road from where he came. Nathan watched as the car disappeared into the distance, the rear door suddenly swinging open as the car wrapped around a sharp curve, as if the taxi was saying good-bye in its own special way.

"Fucking deathtrap," he whispered under his breath as he turned and proceeded down the beaten path that functioned as a main street. Native children were already gathering at his feet, the older ones holding their hands out while the younger ones stared at a distance with large, brown eyes. None of them had shoes, and all of them wore coarse, woolen shirts graced at times with the odd Western reject. He smiled knowingly at the red shirt with the Patriot's football emblem squarely in the center and the decree, "Super bowl champions 2008-the undefeated season!"

A tall boy about twelve made his way through the crowd, knowingly pushing away the closest and shooing away the youngest. Softly he grabbed Nathan's hand and led him down the street, the gang of children following discreetly, giggling occasionally in the high soprano of youth and talking amongst themselves.

Nathan could only be led, his shoes slapping against the sloped earthen path as he glanced around him at the huts that seemed to thicken and crowd the street. Some had wicker doors, similar to the material of the huts themselves. Others had open doorways, and he could glimpse into the darkened, single room of the hut, catching a moving shadow or a pair of whitened eyes set deep into a dark, wrinkled face.

He noticed small stands along the way with small fruit and white tubers of some sort displayed on the counters. Small faggots of grain appeared to be collected and placed in small decorative jars, where their inflorescences blended into different textures and colors. Reed baskets held assorted nuts and vegetables while men stood about in silence, staring at the newcomer being paraded through the street like a captured jungle animal.

As they progressed deeper into the village, the huts and stands became denser. Reaching an especially large stand where a crowd was gathered around a thin strand of a man, seemingly overwhelmed by a thick, black shirt. It hovered over him like a shadow, making his brown complexion darker and the thin, white cigarette stuck between his fingers that much more pronounced.

Presented in front of the man, the young boy spoke directly and strongly in his own dialect as the man listened, glancing occasionally at Nathan. and taking long draws on his cigarette.

Suddenly the boy stopped, and all eyes turned to Nathan.

"Why did you come here?" the man asked in heavily accented English.

"I've come to look for my son," Nathan said and then quickly slipped the picture out of the plastic tag and showed it to the man as evidence of his sincerity. The man took the photograph with two reed-like fingers and astonishingly pink fingernails. With delicacy, he turned it for the other men to see, and one gentleman seemed to move closer and nod. Silently he turned away and slipped behind the others.

"Have you seen him?" Nathan asked, nervous with anticipation.

"Perhaps," the man said. "There are very few Americans that come through here. Was this some time ago?"

Nathan gave a sharp, impatient nod in agreement.

"You need to come back tomorrow. We will have an answer for you." He then handed the picture back to Nathan.

"I would like to ask the other villagers if they have seen him."

"There is no need," the man said, placing the cigarette on the side of his mouth. "Everyone who needs to see it has seen it. I assume you need a place to stay. Please follow this boy, and he will take you to his home for the night and then bring you back in the morning."

With a nod, the boy took Nathan's hand and tried to lead him away. Nathan rejected the hand and moved closer to the tribal leader, only to be confronted by a sudden wall of brawn as the men around him closed him off. "Where's my son!" he screamed. "God damn—if you know where he is, tell me!" Nathan felt lightheaded from the frustration, and the stress made the clouds in his head darken. A headache was brewing, a bad one, but he had to push to seek an answer. All of the travelling and anticipation had reached a boiling point, and it rushed out like steam from a kettle. He heard his voice now stretched and thin, pleading in desperation. "Please, dear God, please at least let me know if he's alive."

Waiting for the emotion to pass, the chief answered in a calm, measured voice. "I cannot tell you because I do not know. There are many secrets here, both in the village and in the mountains around us. Some

I can pass to you, and others I cannot because not even I know of them. This may be a secret you have to discover for yourself. Tomorrow I will let you know all there is to know."

The boy once again took Nathan's hand and proceeded to lead an emotionally limp Nathan out of the hut.

The shack where the boy lived wasn't far from the tribal elders' gathering place. Slipping through the darkened entryway, Nathan's eyes quickly adjusted to a spacious living area with thick woven mats covering the bare floor, and tightly woven wicker walls sectioning the rear of the hut into personal sleeping areas. Seated inside were three native women, one appearing in her fifties that he guessed to be the grandma, and the other two in their thirties. The elder woman was beginning to set up a large metal kettle. Its sides were thick with soot, and its circular handle had been slowly bent into an oval from years of cooking over a hot fire. One of the younger women had already set up the hook and trellis that the pot was to stand on, and was beginning to assemble the wood and tinder for a fire. The remaining women had laid out the fruit and other vegetables for the evening.

Upon his arrival, the three of them immediately stopped and stared at him, a surprising newcomer to their home. The boy spouted out a sharp line of dialect, at which everyone then looked at the eldest member of the family. With soft, contemplating eyes, she looked at Nathan as if trying to see an edge on his rounded soul.

Satisfied, she nodded, and the women contained their work while the boy disappeared behind one of the screens. He appeared a moment later with a collection of skins woven and stuffed to create a thick blanket. Walking over to a vacant corner in the hut, he threw the armload down with a loud thump, pointed at the pile and then at Nathan, and pantomimed a sleeping position with his eyes closed and his hands together. Nathan smiled, and realizing he had been understood, the boy smiled back, his teeth neat and white. One of the younger women, presumably his mother, barked a few quick words, which he responded to quickly by trotting over to some large woven baskets, pushing aside their tops and removing additional quantities of the fruits and vegetables already assembled by the fire.

Feeling the migraine progress at a rapid pace, he threw his duffel down in a heap by the bedding, pushed the blanket around until it looked comfortable, and then flopped down on it with such force, it drew the attention of the grandmother. She eyed him warily as she lifted the assembled pot with both hands, revealing long, sinewy arms and skin drawn tight from years of lifting up the same pot.

As if on cue, two teenage boys stumbled in with what appeared to be four large, skinned rabbits and a collection of snares. Across their shoulders were pelts, similar in size and color to the pelts he was laying on. A slight breeze pushed the smell into the hut, and Nathan recognized the rough, brutal smell of freshly dressed game. It was a smell he was familiar with from when he used to hunt with his father and dress out the pheasants and rabbits that they had killed on his uncle's farm. The contrast of the horrid smell of a skinned pheasant in the barn turned into a pleasant aroma of a perfectly baked bird with a hint of cilantro and sweet potato dressing on the side, topped off with fried green beans and a red onion garnish. It was the disparity that led to the curiosity that bred the passion to cook. And the passion was rising again as his professional curiosity began to awaken. He hoped the awakening wasn't diluted by the wolf of a migraine lurking in the backwoods of his brain, so he tried to focus as much as he could on the process in front of him.

Intrigued, he watched as the grandmother poured a sizable amount of water into the empty pot, followed by the fruit and vegetables each were preparing. Placed out of sight of the grandmother were small pots of herbs. As the daughters were contributing their share, the grandmother reached behind her and took out small fingertip amounts of each herb, which she then threw into the pot.

In the meantime, the boys had sat down near the newly started fire and began to sectionalize the carcasses. Sharp cracks were heard as joints were snapped back to free limbs, and with small knives taken from their loose packets, they dressed out the breast and some of the back meat. As the boys worked, the air became more pungent. And the atmosphere became more charged as the pieces of the first two were thrown into the pot, the empty ribcages and heads placed lengthwise in a nice row by the entrance. The pot could only hold enough to cook half the food, so when the contents reached the rim, the grandmother produced a flat wooden spoon from somewhere in her cloak and held it briefly over the pot like a witch before the cauldron. Then, delicately she pushed the meat deeper into the stew as if coaxing the animal into a cage. When the meat had disappeared into the broth, she gave the pot two revolutions, tapped the spoon on the rim, and slipped it back into her cloak.

The remaining meat and vegetables were on a mat by the fire. As the meal cooked, the boys disappeared out the door of the hut but did not go far. He could hear their chatter from his lounging position on the furs. The two daughters began weaving on separate mats as the grandmother began to arrange the spice pots into a specific order, keeping one eye on the pot as the bubbles began to emerge at the top.

The hut was now gaining an earthly, smoked atmosphere as the meal began to cook, and the smell of bitter spices and sweet fruit began to swell the air in the hut. He could almost recognize some—a lime, but not quite. Sweet potato, or close to it. Cumin, almost. As his curiosity grew, he finally decided to take the bold step of walking over to the fire and finding out exactly what each was.

Struggling to get up, partly from the stretch of lying down and partly from the migraine beginning to knock his balance off, he stunned everyone in the hut by walking over and kneeling by the fire. The warmth seemed to help stabilize him, and as he knelt there, he motioned to the grandmother for the spoon. She glared at him with raw, steely eyes. They were a dark green and made her appear much harsher than she actually was as she gave up the spoon and sat passively as he turned the contents of the pot. Hoping to taste some of the blend, he pooled a little into the spoon and attempted to bring it close to his mouth. When it was close enough that he could feel the heat on his lips, he felt a sharp smack on his wrist, strong enough to leave a sting and slip the contents off of the spoon. Turning to look at his antagonist, he saw the old woman staring at him with a tight chin and creased eyes. Holding another spoon in the air before him, he took the warning seriously and slowly returned his utensil to the pot, secretly wondering how many spoons she could possibly hold in that cloak of hers.

The meat was already softening, but the tubers and the fruit still seemed to be whole and undaunted. After some time, the grandmother dipped her spoon into the broth and offered it to him. Apparently he hadn't broken a rule of etiquette but one of privilege.

Reluctantly, he blew on it slightly and tasted just a little off the end. It was as rough as it smelled, with each flavor fighting for dominance, while in his mind the rules of open-pit cooking and their application were being debated and applied. Taking a second

161

dip of his own utensil, he came to some conclusions, verified some absolutes, and developed a process.

Motioning toward the spices and to some other open bowls, the grandmother, equally intrigued, presented him with all the open jars she had and watched as he smelled each one, savoring the aroma, even putting a little on the end of his tongue to gauge the flavor and body. In the last bowl, he was lucky enough to find the last ingredient he would need. Reaching for an empty bowl, he poured out a little of what appeared to be a sort of wheat flour. Next, he reached over to the mat where the fruit and tubers were and selected three of the plumpest specimens. Reaching into his pocket, he pulled out his buck knife and split them in half, squeezing the juice into the flour. When he felt he had enough, he created a slurry, using two of his fingers to push the lumps out and create a smooth paste.

Next, he took one of the back legs of the rabbit, if that was what it really was, and one of the tubers. He examined the tuber carefully and realized it was more like a yucca than a potato. He hesitated as a wave of pain pulsed through. Regaining his train of thought, he used his knife to slit a deep trench, almost a pocket, into the thickest part of the thigh. Shaving off a palm full of shavings from the tuber, he then pushed it into the pocket until it was full but not too dense. He pushed the seams of the meat together as best he could. The meat was a little sinewy, and that helped to keep the incision closed.

Next, he took a fingertip full of a spice that was almost like thyme, yet with a thicker, longer-lasting aftertaste. Rubbing it into the thigh, he covered as much as he could without overwhelming the meat. It would be easy to overpower the taste of the game; however, having never really eaten wild rat, that may be what they were reaching for. Another wave of pain shot through, and he closed his eyes until it receded. When he opened them, both of the daughters were now engrossed in what he was doing, while the grandmother had disappeared. The question of where she went was answered as he heard a fumbling of mats behind a partition in the back. She burst out and within a few quick steps was kneeling beside him. In one hand, she held a clutch of thin branches, while with the other she motioned for his knife. He passed it to her, and after she had taken a full measure of his frame, she reached behind his head and placed a surprisingly warm, calloused hand on his neck. As she looked into his eyes, instantly she nodded. The position of her hand was lower than where the pain was, so he moved it up higher, to the base of his skull, and then nodded in return.

Laying the branches on her lap, she pulled out a medium-sized twig and cut it into a half-inch length. She pointed to the piece of stick and then to her pink, exposed gums. Picking up on the intent quickly, he took the piece from her and did as he was instructed, sliding the hard piece of wood between his lip and gum, notching it in firmly with his tongue. With this primal medicine ritual completed, he returned to his meal, wondering if this would match the LSD highs of his youth or just knock him out for a few days so he couldn't mess with their food. In his last act, he used his two fingers to cover the thigh with his homemade rub. When that was completed, he reached for one of the branches the boys had used as a snare and pierced the thigh at the seam. He could now hold the meat over the fire like a hot dog, completing the assembly by jabbing the sticks end far into the ground so it dangled only a few inches above the fire.

With that accomplished, Nathan returned to his small nest of furs and waited until the meat cooked through. By now, the full flavor of the stick in his mouth was beginning to seep into the salivary glands, and its rich chalky flavor began to drift into his nostrils, causing his olfactory system to be overwhelmed by the musk. Feeling the root slip a little, he stuck his fingers between his gum and lip and pulled out the saturated piece of branch. He could taste the sweetness from his fruit paste concoction on his fingers, but he could not actually feel his fingers in his mouth. As he pulled the twig out, he felt along the gum with his other fingers and noticed that where the root had been lodged, it was completely numb, and luckily only there. Glancing at the stem in his fingers, he was taken aback by the green barbs that had turned to brown, with an orangey sap oozing out of the ends. It was very soft and malleable now, and as he squeezed it, the orange color became more brilliant and thicker.

Out of the corner of his eye, he noticed the old woman smiling with a large gap-toothed grin. She nodded approvingly, tapping her head as she gazed at him. True enough, the migraine had receded. No waves, no sharp pangs, or angry punches. It was there, he could feel it, but it was a dull hum, much like an engine far off in the distance.

When his meat had finished, he pulled it off the stake carefully, due to the hot rub. At the same time, the stew was also presented, and each shared what they had with the others around them. The meat hadn't cooked evenly due to the fire, but there was enough cooked through that he could ascertain what the taste would be like. It definitely had the spike of game and hardened texture of a wild animal, but it was decidedly sweet initially with a fading bitter aftertaste. It needed to be improved and was very original—definitely something he could bring home. The rat would be hard to get in the United states (domesticated, that is), but the fruits and vegetables must be from somewhere. Rabbit would be a good substitute. Nathan taught the boys how to set up the meal, and in return, more stew was prepared. When one of them seemed to be asking what the new meal was called, Nathan could only smile and say BBQ. Easy and to the point. In turn, Nathan asked about the other ingredients, writing down the phonetics so he knew how to ask for them when he got back to the States.

When the meal was done, Nathan lay back on his mats and was prepared to pull out maps and descriptions that he might need to be ready for tomorrow. Suddenly, however, he felt tired and depleted. The longer he lay on the mats, the more prone he became and the more distant the voices. Soon he was in a deep sleep, coaxed by the warmth and the softness, and oblivious to the thin line of orange salvia slipping down the corner of his mouth and into a small pool on the curled rabbit pelt beside his head.

The chattering and squealing of the village children slowly brought him out of a dream. In it, he was with Steven as a young boy, perhaps twelve, and they were walking along a train platform, looking at the different cars and engines. He could almost feel the grasp of the young boy's hand in his, soft and curious. The palm warm with the love of a son. Then suddenly it was gone, and he could feel a cold wind blow through it. Staring at the empty hand, he turned around to see Steven standing in the doorway of a long, steel passenger car. He was older and dressed as a tropical adventurer, with rough oily hair and a beard of four days slowly growing over his chin and jaw.

As the train was pulling away, he heard him yell, "I'm okay, Dad! I'll always be okay!" And he waved a long wave with an outstretched arm and smiled that lazy smile he had. As the noise of the train and commuters around him rose, he blinked himself awake and realized the noise around him had pulled him back.

Along his cheeks, he could still feel the warmth of the tears he had cried as his own private movie showed in his head. He felt rested, almost serene, and the anxiety that the fear and worry seemed to feed had abated. He now knew that his son was dead.

Rising slowly, he gazed around the room. There was a haze from the fire the previous night, and it amplified the stillness. He appeared to be alone, but the sudden appearance of the grandmother added sudden vibrancy to the space.

"Alha!" she hissed as he shuffled to stand. She immediately went over to the cold pot by the fire to offer him the leftovers from the night before, but before she could spoon the stew into a bowl, he made it very clear he wasn't interested.

"Rat," he declared, "good supper, just not for breakfast." He pushed them away with two open palms and a strong shake of the head. Reaching into his duffel, he pulled out some jerky and a canteen of water. Making a very visible effort to take a large bite and drink a huge swallow of water, he was able to effectively persuade her to return it to the pot, lay the empty bowl down, and disappear behind the palisades of wicker.

Having taken a few bites and swallows, he slipped the jerky into his breast pocket and tossed the canteen into his duffel. Once again, she burst into the room with such immediacy that Nathan hesitated. What could she have now? Fruit bat cheese? Pine nut crackers? Perhaps millipede twirls in a warm agave sauce? She presented him with a large bundle of stems, similar to the ones last night that alleviated the migraine. Smiling, he willingly took them and tried to express his gratitude by holding her hand firmly and looking straight into her pale green eyes. She smiled at the appreciation.

The chatter outside ceased, and the scene was interrupted by his young guide coming through the door. Smiling, he motioned for Nathan to follow him, which he did after hastily closing his duffel bag and scooping it under his arm.

The morning sun blinded him slightly, and he hesitated for a moment. When his eyes had adjusted, the town leader stood before him in a bright orange shirt, straw hat, and long billowed trousers. His minions gathered around were him standing in much the same order as the other day.

"I trust that you slept well?" he asked.

"Good," Nathan uttered. "Now what have you got for me?"

"In the hills there are many temples and caves that were used by our early ancestors. My people tell me your son came here to look for them. He went up the path into the mountains. No one here saw him come back down."

"Did anyone go to look for him?" Nathan asked.

"People come and go as they please. There are other paths and other villages in the mountains.

Like a *pantiqua*, he may go in one hole and come out another."

Motioning for the boy to come in front of him, which he did obediently, he then placed both hands on his shoulders. "He will show you where the trail begins. Be careful," he said, holding up one finger as a warning. "This trail is old and broken in many places."

Nathan nodded in understanding, but he had already tied up his duffel and placed it on his back. Securing the support belt to take the weight off, he now motioned for the boy to lead on. Brushing past the elders without another word, he followed his young guide through the tight maze of huts and streets. Apparently he did not have the attention of the village anymore, as there were no children following and no curious looks from the elders.

After some time, they reached the far side of the village where they were confronted with a thick wall of foliage. Reaching in, the boy pulled away a thin trunk with thick palm-like leaves. As if opening a secret door, a beaten path of polished stepping stones on the other side of the foliage led further into the woods. Ending his appointed mission, the boy then pointed into the jungle and smiled softly. Taking this as his cue, Nathan smiled back, patted him firmly on the head, and disappeared into the wild.

The outer foliage of the jungle was incredibly thick, and it took a great deal of effort to push his way through the green mass if only for just a few feet. Vines tangled his feet, and large fronds flew from entanglements to blind him and try to push him back into the clearing. But as the effort was beginning to strain him, he pushed through the last palm stand, only to emerge in a long clearing remarkably free of thick foliage. On the outskirts, there was abundant sunlight, and the plant material grew freely. But inside the jungle, where the mature trees guarded the forest floor and allowed the sunlight to peek through sparingly, and the rainfall to appear in drizzles, the undergrowth was held in check, although ready at any instant to emerge upon any overflow of sunlight.

The way was clear enough that a paved path of rough, grey bricks led up and away from the edge. They were thick with moss and at times pushed uneven by roots and sapling growth, but they were true in their path. The centuries of elements had cracked and chipped away the corners, and he could see where weaknesses in the base of the stone had caused washouts and sinkholes. But the tread of thousands of feet seemed to have imbedded them deeper into the structure of the mountain, such that it did not appear to be a path leading to a temple, but a series of vertebrate leading up the spine of the mountain. Taking a deep breath, Nathan shouldered the backpack to a more comfortable position and ascended.

With each stride, he opened his mind to everything he passed. Trying to assume where his son could have gone, he looked for broken branches, shreds of clothing, footprints, perhaps a discarded water bottle, anything to tell him he was on the right path. Closing his eyes, he tried to think as his son, relive what he was looking for, assume where he would leave the path, or just stay on it until it reached a remote village or a geographical dead end. Then where to? He tried not to think that far ahead, only concentrate on the environment around him.

Stopping on occasion, he would take a sip of water. He used it sparingly since a refill point was unknown. He also took a few bites of the jerky to keep his strength up. Around him, the artifacts of an ancient civilization were spread out like thrown chess pieces. Half-buried hands as large as he was were adjacent to the worn, eroding statures that once held them. Heads of serpents and cougars as large as him glared back at him as he walked the path around them. Abandoned centuries ago, the jungle was slowly reclaiming them with the patience of endless time.

It was after three or four hours of hiking that he came to a large break in the path. A large tree had fallen from a few hundred yards up the ridge and tumbled down across the path, carrying with it a huge section of the path and knocking down the smaller trees in its path. The seeds in waiting had already sprung to life, each of the trees struggling to reach beyond the others to be the solitary climax tree and slowly starve the competitors of light and water.

The tree was enormous. Lying on its side, the trunk was about five feet tall, the path beyond with thick, broken branches and oversized leaves of over-achieving new growth. Concluding that this was the best place to rest, he discovered the head of a warrior god half buried in the soil, its mouth howling in indignity as if disgusted with its final resting place.

Unloading his duffel and placing his water bottle in the soldier's ear, Nathan retrieved from the side pocket the fruit he had accumulated and took a bite of what appeared to be a green peach. He knew he was going to reach a crossroad soon, as to whether to continue forward and take his chances at finding another village for the night, or turn around and head back to return to the village before nightfall. In his exuberance when starting, he neglected to realize he had no camping gear and barely enough food for two days. Perhaps a return to the camp and hiring a guide would be the best method. While he was contemplating this, he bit past the rind and suddenly felt a cold sweat on his back, and his arms and legs went numb.

As if in pity for his anguish, the forest lying serenely before him was revealing one of its secrets. Before him, perhaps twenty yards, Nathan noticed a small piece of metal glinting in the sunlight. It was barely visible, but the hole in the forest canopy allowed enough light in that it was readily apparent from the angle he was sitting. Like a small star, it gleamed brilliantly. He stared at it, barely breathing as if daring it to move, and then he tossed the fruit aside and began a slow descent using the branches of the fallen tree as a brace.

Reaching the piece of metal sticking out of the soil, he grabbed the most exposed edge and pulled gently. Having rested in the duff for some time, it resisted at first and then released its grip on the soil. The piece of metal came out slowly, as did the two arm bones it was attached to.

When Steven was thirteen, he liked to jump out of his swing at its highest point and then land on the ground and roll like a paratrooper. During one of those jumps, his thumb became entangled in the swing chain, so when he jumped, the swing pulled him back, throwing off his balance and timing. Instead of landing on his feet and pitching into a roll, he instead landed on his arm, breaking it.

The plate Nathan cradled carefully in his hands was the same plate the doctor showed him before they implanted it in Steven's arm. "It'll never move or come loose," the doctor assured him. "It will be in place forever." How right he was, Nathan thought.

He spent the night on the path, curled up in the small sleeping bag he had in the duffle. Sleeping relatively well, knowing that Steven was close by, seemed to make up for the occasional scurrying of the night animals. At dawn, he arose and began the excavation. He had to dig under the trunk to get most of the upper torso. The ribs and other bones were crushed into small pieces, and he sifted through the soil and rotten undergrowth to find as much as he could. Staying throughout the day, he unearthed the full skeleton along with a belt buckle, a pen, shoe eyelets, and a few shirt buttons. The forest had claimed all that it could, but Nathan was determined to make the rest his own. Finally, his hands and forearms black with forest duff, he gazed at the pile of bones that was once his son. He wanted to cry, felt as if there were words of absolution to be said. Shouts of anger to be heard, tantrums of sorrow to be bled out.

But he felt none of that now. Just a quiet resilience to finish what he came here for.

"I love you, Steven," he said to the stack of yellowing bones.

He had recovered Steven's old school backpack from the duffel, and he now opened it up as wide as it could go.

"Let's go home," he said softly as he gently picked up each piece, as if they were crystal itself, and placed it in the bag.

Vanessa's letter

—•—

VANESSA STOOD AND WATERED THE new flowerbeds at the front of the house absentmindedly. She had just planted the line of marigolds the weekend before, neatly lined in front of the evergreens that graced the entrance to the yellow brick of her mother's bungalow, but the sudden heat of an early summer had begun to dry out the flowers before they had time to establish. Tucked neatly against the large globed yews at the entrance to the small house, they stood straight as soldiers, obediently taking their cue to stand at attention with a solid display of bright orange on their epaulets, yet visibly suffering from the arid soil. Despite the hanging leaves, she knew they would respond quickly to the water, just as the grass was reaching mowing height at a record pace. Her mother would have done the work eventually—at seventy-eight, she was still able to bend and pull—but Vanessa had time, and the work was a form of therapy.

The sun felt nice on the back of her neck, having pulled her long, black hair into a ponytail high on the back of her head. The weather allowed her to pull out her most comfortable khaki shorts and a worn blue T-shirt she had dedicated to yard work. It took a while to find them, but the worn tennis shoes that were a

Greg Wright

part of the seasonal requirement were located far in the back of her basement closet at home.

Despite the distraction of being outdoors and in the environment she loved, she would sometimes catch herself drifting away. Sometimes she would jerk suddenly when she saw the water intended for the flowers puddling at her feet. It was during one of these fading-away episodes that she failed to hear the postman as he strode up the walk toward the porch.

Startled, she jumped at his greeting.

"Sorry, Vanessa, I didn't mean to startle you." He chuckled as he finished sorting out the bundles into two groups of small business envelopes and a group of flyers, newspapers, and a large white envelope.

"It's okay, Peter," she replied. "I seem to be more and more distracted these days."

"It's no wonder," he said, lowering his voice. "I heard about Oscar, and I'm truly sorry. I met him a few times, and he really seemed to be a nice man. How long were you married?"

"Twenty-two years."

"A generation."

"Yes, and it has been a difficult three weeks . . ." She let the sentence trail off, not sure how it should end.

Quickly he changed the subject. "I see you planted flowers. Nice touch so early."

"Thanks. My mom loves orange, and marigolds are her favorite."

"Is she home?" he asked, starting to shift from leg to leg with the growing impatience of completing a job half done.

"No, she's not. My sister, Valerie, is also at work," she added for no apparent reason.

"Okay," he said cheerfully. "And since you're here, would you like me to give you yours?"

"Sure." Since she lived only a few blocks away, he already had the bundle in his bag and readily pulled it out. Handing her both bundles, hers much thicker than her mother's, the postman stood there a few seconds longer, not quite sure how to finish the conversation. Dropping the hose in the grass, she took both bundles with both hands and glanced through them for only a second before smiling back at the postman.

"I noticed there are a lot of condolence letters from all over the country. It seems Oscar was well known."

"Yes," she said as she shifted the thick pile of twenty or so letters. The thought of going through them and reliving the pain of the funeral and the burden of grief caused her shoulders to sag slightly.

Perhaps she would get to them later. An "I'm sorry for your loss" doesn't need an immediate response.

"Oscar sold industrial machinery, and it took him everywhere. He was very likeable."

"Did you travel with him a lot?"

"Oh yes, quite frequently. I went everywhere he went, except for Texas."

"Why not Texas?"

"I don't know really. I guess it just never appealed to me. Just nothing there I wanted to see. He always went on his own, and he never seemed to mind."

That awkward silence appeared again as she drifted over a fragment of a memory that had breezed into her mind.

"Well, got to finish my route," he remarked, shifting his bag higher on his shoulder. "And if there is anything I can do, just let me know. Okay?" With a weak smile and a sad expression of regret, he strode away, leaving her standing silently.

"Good-bye," she quickly said, despite the fact he was already six strides away and sorting for his next parcel. Deciding now was as good a time as any for a break, she walked up the front steps and into the modest three-bedroom house. There was a small entryway with another door only six feet past the main entrance, and when she was a child, she and the other neighborhood children would pretend it was a space lock between the ship and the universe. She rarely played this game with boys, but Valerie always did.

Entering through the front door, she passed through a narrow foyer that spilled into a living room. The antiquated recliners, quilts, formations of picture frames, and a ticking grandfather clock identified this as her mother's realm. A sanctuary of memories and the preservation of the familial status quo was the intent, and this was established quite well. As cluttered as it seemed, there was some order to it all. On the end tables were the pictures of the parents—her mother and long-deceased father—and a few with Vanessa and Valerie as children on the mantel. Also on the mantel was more of the distant family history—grandfathers, grandmothers, aunts, uncles, and the lineage that preceded them. There were a few of her and her sister, but only as young children and as props for the residuals. Bookends for the classics, she used to tell Oscar.

Over on the piano were the offspring pieces. A few of Valerie, but mostly photos of her and Oscar on one of their many trips, each photo frame reflective of the location. Key West had the aqua-blue frame with fake shells in the corners. Wyoming had a picture of them on horses with a frame made of rawhide. In California under the giant sequoias, a frame of redwood, and when they were skiing in Colorado, a white plastic frame with snowflakes and a miniature pair of skies bisecting the top corner of the frame. This photo she lingered over, as it was the only one with Oscar, herself, her sister, Valerie, and Valerie's boyfriend, Neil. It had been taken many years ago, and she still didn't remember why Valerie went, only that Neil was the new love helping her get over the old boyfriend, a name she couldn't recall if her life depended on it. She didn't remember seeing him much after that trip, as Valerie was surely on to the next one before the plane landed. Mixed with the pictures were the small souvenirs she brought back, as if the photographs weren't enough validation.

As she walked through the living room, she entered a dining room of equal size. Walking deeper into the house, she entered another small hallway where there were two bedrooms, one for her mother, which was more of a memory tomb than the living room, and a guestroom that was rarely used for company but used frequently by her when Oscar was away. During the times she chose not to go with him, she would stay here rather than by herself in their empty house a few blocks away. With no children in the marriage, her time was her own.

Across the hallway was a bathroom, and next to it was a small staircase leading to the upstairs. The upstairs had two large bedrooms, one of which her sister now occupied, and a small sunroom in the back of the house that was used as a sleeper porch in the days before air-conditioning. She and Valerie lived there as girls, and when she was older and engaged, she moved out, surrendering the upstairs to her younger sister.

Another bathroom was located between the rooms, allowing for Valerie to be completely independent of the downstairs with the exception of meals.

The second floor was now Valerie's realm. Having never had the need or desire to settle down, she just made a home here. It didn't seem to bother her mom. Despite her vigor, she could barely get up the stairs anyway, and as long as Valerie respected the house, this was the way it was to stay. Her sister's needs were very different from hers, and as long as the boundaries were set, there was never a conflict. Reaching the kitchen, she tried to set her bundles on the thin-legged, stainless steel table, but the bundles slipped from her fingers and fell to the floor in a disorganized mess. With a heavy sigh, she bent over and collected them. Then she stacked them in one big pile on the corner of the table.

She went to the cupboard for a glass, selecting one with a faded pattern of yellow and white palm fronds, and then clicked in some ice from the door dispenser on the refrigerator. Having poured a glass of lemonade, she squeezed between the edge of the table and the chair at the end next to the letters. Quickly she sorted through the letters, initially sorting between hers and her mother's, and then mentally filing them under trash, bereavement, and bills. Once this was completed, she set to work reading and deciphering them. First on the list was to open the large envelope from the post office that didn't seem to fit the other categories. It was addressed to the occupant of the house and was incredibly light and couldn't have carried anything important.

Reaching over to the long, metal letter opener that was permanently assigned to the napkin holder in the center of the table, she adeptly slit the envelope open at the end and reached in for the contents. Pulling out the form letter of apology from the post office, she skimmed through it quickly and then laid it down as she glimpsed into the surgically split end of the envelope. Cautiously, she reached in and pulled out a small envelope that was discolored badly by mold and some sort of grease, as if it had been left under a worn doormat for a winter.

Gazing intently, she could make out that it was to V. Lederman, but the postmark was horribly smudged, and the return address seemed to have been in a lighter ink, making it almost a shadow. Focusing intently, she stared at the lettering when suddenly, as if he had whispered in her ear himself, she saw it was from Oscar.

Letting the letter slip through her hands, she watched it fall directly to the table with a slap. She rubbed her chest to calm a heart that was pounding. When they were dating, Oscar wrote to her frequently, writing words from his heart that were like a salve to her loneliness. Now here was another, presented to her by fate, as if giving her some sort of consolation at taking her husband away.

With shaking hands, she slit open the end with the opener, and in her unsteadiness, nicked the end of her thumb with the sharp end. After she put her lips to the bleeding cut, she pulled out the folded pages, as dry and crisp as papyrus itself, and laid it before her, hoping to awaken words she thought she would never read again.

My love,

As I am writing, my concentration becomes blurred by thoughts of you. They rush past so quickly it becomes difficult to keep focused as I can still hear the sound of your voice, and its trance upon me pulls me away, causing me to gaze into the empty distance and smile. I must appear contented and happy when I walk because people I don't even know smile back and return the light in my eyes that is only there because of you.

When I walk, my hand instinctively reaches for yours, and it aches for your touch. I close my eyes and dream of burying my face into your hair, breathing the scent of you and pushing your red curls against my face like so many fresh picked flowers. Right now I just wish to kiss you as hard and true as lovers should. A kiss that is so deep we both blend together in spirit and flesh and remain so until an eternity passes. Until we blend like two sands poured into each other, so completely and finely matched as to make a new whole. Let the searing heat of our passion fuse it together to create one single crystalizing sculpture, pure and unblemished in its true form, and forever glimmering. Until we stop living in these two worlds we have and just disappear into one joyous mold, creating our own world, then we will be happy.

The weekend we spent skiing together was time spent with you that I will always cherish. Despite us all skiing as a group, I could only focus on you. The one run we took together, alone in the solitude of a pine forest, the only sound being our skis in the uncut powder, was how I wish we could always be. Knowing you are with me fires the tempest in my chest, abates the despair and loneliness I feel when you are absent, and fills my soul with richness, a euphoria that I have never experienced.

I know you feel this way also because at the end of the run, as we sipped the hot wine while warming in the hot tub, I felt your leg next to mine, I took a chance and laced my hand on your thigh unseen under the bubbling water. As I felt you lean toward me, my heart leapt at just the sense of your interest.

She had to stop reading as her hand had begun to cover her mouth, and her breathing was again becoming short and hard. The cut on her thumb still stung as she rose from the chair, stumbling away, and headed for the bathroom. Turning the water on at the sink, she let it flow until it began to pool by the drain and then slowly eased back on the valve until it was a solid column. With a quick scoop of her hands, she doused the cool water over her face, and the shock seemed to calm her nerves. Reaching for the nearest bath towel, she dabbed her face and tried to dry off the water that had spilled onto her shirt.

Opening the medicine cabinet, she scanned for the peroxide and bandages and then pulled each one out as she discovered them. Rinsing the wound out, she could envision the hot tub there before her, as if gazing into a miniature bowl of time, each participant in their place, the letter a script of what was playing out before her. Dressing the wound, she could imagine scooping out someone and throwing them into the hard cold desert of the tub, or using the back of her hand, splashing them all out as if in the act of a vengeful god.

Finishing the first aid, she turned the water off but left the materials on the counter. Returning to the table, she stood next to it as she used both hands to bring the letter within reading distance of her eyes.

> *I remember drinking the wine in one swallow, closing my eyes and imagining that it was just the two of us in the dark, that we could shed our clothes and I could fold you completely in my arms, hold you tightly in a forever grip of my muscle and bone, such that I could feel your heart beating against my chest. We would be there alone hidden by a screen of steam from the bath. A fusion of our primal spirits as we enter a*

new world. I long to bury my nose deep into your neck to breathe in the warmth of your skin and to kiss away the sweet sweat. I long to feel the pull of our legs wrapped around me, heels locked behind my back, never wanting to let go. A chain pulling me into your depths, a journey I could only dream of and whose fulfillment could only end my life because nothing that could happen to me afterwards could ever bring me such joy and elation.

It is here I must stop. I could write on into the night and for days afterwards, but I must get some sleep. Tomorrow is Los Angeles, Thursday is Kansas City, and Monday is Dallas. This business that I am in provides well, but the penalty is to be away from home too much.

I will sleep sound tonight knowing that I have purged my soul of what aches in me. This burning desire for you has been sated, but the beating of my lonely longing heart keeps on. Knowing that I will see you again keeps me going, but with each day, as the longing grows stronger, my hope is to see you again.

Help me ease these feelings and meet me in Dallas. You have before, and the time alone with you is priceless. Just the sound of you breathing next to me as we sleep at night gives me such peace, and it gives me hope as this endless travelling draws to a close.

You are deepest in my heart, and I think of you always.

Oscar

Finishing the letter, she placed it open on the table. She reached up and rubbed her eyes slowly, feeling the rough edge of the band aid against her eyelid, yet craving the relief the sensation brought. *It is the emotion*, she kept telling herself. *It is the emotion in his phrases and his descriptions.* She could feel his passion as if he were right in front of her, holding her as tightly as possible, and kissing her tenderly on the neck.

Placing her hands on the back of the chair, she opened her eyes, still watery from the pressure of her fingers, and with that sensation, she wanted to cry. She so desperately wanted to cry, to match his emotive power with hers like two titans fighting for control of the seas. But she couldn't. She couldn't even will it. If he were there, it would come fast enough, a physical power he could see. But he wasn't there; he could never be there again. So the tears wouldn't come.

Regaining her sight, she calmly walked into the living room, very steady, very controlled. She had to call someone. As she sat down at the end of the sofa, she reached for the cordless phone in the carriage on the end table. There was only one person to call, and with the quick jabs of both thumbs, the number dashed out into tones that then paused when she put the receiver to her ear.

On the third ring, there was a click, a second's pause, and then a woman' voice.

"Castaway Siding. Valerie speaking."

"Val, it's Vanessa."

"God, Vanessa, you sound terrible. Are you okay?"

"Well . . . no. You need to come home as soon as you can."

"What is it? God—is it Mom?"

"No, no it isn't Mom. It's just that there's a letter that came in the mail. And it . . . it . . . is for you."

Deborah's Letter

---·●·---

As HE WAS GETTING OFF of the train, the cold January wind seared across his face, causing him to bury his chin deeper into the wool collar of his winter coat. Preparing to depart, he pushed his cotton cap down tighter and felt the grip on his suitcase grow stronger as he focused on the station house just a few hundred yards away. Jumping off the steel stairs, he concentrated on getting there even though he had his share of interferences, including the mother greeting her daughter from college and the egregiously old couple struggling to get off the train, afraid of being trapped and sent to Lincoln, the next station.

Dodging and sidestepping to avoid them, he made it through the collection of travelers and shuffled quickly into a damp and hardened train depot. There were just as many transients there as outside, but at least the wind was gone, and he could breathe through his nose without feeling like it was closing. Struggling through the mass of Gore-Tex and wool, he finally reached a corner booth, its long, wooden bench and high-backed angle the only refuge in the terminal. Pushing close to the steel box of a radiator, he stared out the large windows at the huge clouds of exhaust coming from the cars and locomotives, people talking to each other as if in a sea of vapor. They seemed oblivious to the conditions, whereas he wondered how in god's name someone want could to live in a place like this.

Actually, at one time, he did. Raised in this very town as a child, he grew up with the cold and heat of the Illinois seasons. As a child, he had wonderful memories of snowball fights, snow forts, and sledding until late at night. But as he grew older and more sophisticated, he began to realize that he didn't have to live this way his entire life. There were actually climates where it never dropped below thirty-two degrees, places where, despite the temperature, the sun would shine, and you could go out, and the sole necessity was a pair of sunglasses.

Finally one day it happened—that moment when all reason seemed to coalesce around a conclusion, when a disturbance reached critical mass, and the time for longing and assumption were to be discarded in place of action. And it occurred at one of the most unlikely times.

He was helping his elderly aunt take some boxes out of her apartment. They weren't heavy, just bulky and awkward, making it difficult to see around. It was just before Easter, and it was becoming one of those winters where there was the tease of spring with a few days of sunshine and warmth, initiating the appearance of the spring tulips and hyacinths. But then an errant cold front brought in four inches of snow and a return to the frigid conditions of the previous four months. Nothing was worse for his depression than the appearance of hope and then having it suddenly dashed and shattered like an icicle on the pavement.

Negotiating around the front door of the retirement complex, he was able to reach the car door when it happened. He stepped toward the door, and his shoe slipped off of the curb into an icy slush pile, hedged up tightly against the curb.

He closed his eyes as the sharp dampness soaked quickly through his shoe and into his sock. Stepping away from the curb, he tried to hop a few steps back, but the barrier had been breached, and the icy cold water prickled his skin until his toes became numb with the chill.

By the time he had retreated inside the doorway and sat down in a chair, his foot felt cold and lifeless. Removing his sock and shoe, he massaged the blue and white flesh until some traces of pink began to show again.

Looking out into the snow-crusted parking lot with its blackened bergs of tire ice festooning the spaces, its chilled crusts of ice and water, and the hardened mountains of snow pushed off of the pavement like glaciers, he realized that the end was now. No more of this, and more importantly, never again. As he gazed up to the snow-blurred sky and at the orange ball of the sun struggling to rescue the tundra below it, he swore an oath to the ball of fire that he would only go where he shined the most, and the godforsaken fingers of winter would never reach him again.

The following day, he told his landlord he was vacating the premises, attached a small trailer to his SUV, and pulled out of the Midwest, turning the slightly upraised hood of his vehicle south, determined not to stop until he reached the Florida border. Reaching it after only a half-dozen stops for fuel, food, and one time in southern Georgia to toss his winter coat, gloves, hat, scarf, and boots into a recycle bin, he took a deep breath of the Florida air.

Establishing himself in Florida was easy. No one who lived there seemed to have been born there. Everyone was a transplant like himself—all of them with similar stories about realizing the insanity of living in a climate that was unbearable for so many months of the year, and their epiphany at reaching the end of tolerance. Finding their oasis of mercurial temperance and an endless dosage of unregulated vitamin D.

For the most part, he kept his vow never to return, breaking on only three occasions—the death of his parents and the birth of his nephew. But now he was back again, replying to the emergency summons of his sister, Trudy, and reinforced by the seriousness expressed by his younger brother, Austin, that there was a situation that needed to be addressed, and it only could be resolved with his attendance.

So here he waited, watching as the other passengers embarked into the arms of their comrades, ready to take them home, or to a restaurant, or to an event and out of the cold. Facing him was a large window that revealed the entire parking lot, and across it he could see thin clouds of exhaust trailing upwards into the sky as the cars maneuvered to work the best angle to get in a line and pass through the exit. It reminded him of a documentary he saw about raising cattle out in the west and the vapor that would arise as they would pack tightly together to ford a stream or fit through a gate.

The sun was making its early winter departure, and he tightened his cap and gloves, anticipating the biting cold, when he felt a touch on his wrist.

"Uncle Jeremy?" a small voice squeaked.

Jeremy turned and looked down on a smiling, red-nosed, seven-year-old boy, who was looking up at him with a scattered-tooth grin and the wild eyes of discovery.

"Todd," Jeremy replied, smiling, bending over to give the boy a hug, trying as best as he could to feel his frame amid the layers of fleece.

Breaking away, Todd grabbed his hand and began to lead him away from the window. "Mom is over there by the door, and Dad's got the car just outside so you won't be cold."

True to his word, Jeremy saw his younger sister. She smiled and greeted him with a quick kiss on the cheek. Hustling through the thinning crowd, the three of them slipped out the door and into a warm sedan, with Jeremy and Todd in the back.

Trudy's husband intercepted his bag as he opened the back door, slipped it into the open trunk, and then trotted over to the driver's side. Trudy was already securely in the passenger side when he closed the door, notched the car into gear, and slid the car into the herd struggling through a narrow gate.

As they cautiously made their way through the slow procession of brilliant red taillights, Trudy turned to face the two of them sitting awkwardly side by side, her young son playfully eyeing his uncle with a sideways tilt, Jeremy pressed back as deep into the seat as possible to preserve whatever heat his body was putting out.

"Nice coat!" Trudy purred.

Jeremy squinted at her with contempt. "I will never buy another winter coat, glove, hat, or any such winter garb ever again. I borrowed this from my neighbor, Mrs. Rothberg. It was her husband's, and she never had the heart to give it away after he died. Trust me, immediately after I get back home, the whole ensemble will rest very comfortably on her doorstep."

"Uncle Jeremy?" a small voice interjected.

"Yes?"

"Are you afraid of snow?'

"No, I'm not afraid of snow; I just don't like it." He then turned to his sister. "So what's the family emergency that I had to be here for?"

Trudy dropped her voice and replied, "A letter came."

"A letter? What kind of letter? What did it say?"

Trudy's eyes widened, and she looked at her son and then back at Jeremy. "Let's just say it was long overdue and may answer some questions."

"Uncle Jeremy?"

"Yes," he replied with a heavy sigh.

"Are you afraid of dinosaurs too?"

""No, I'm not afraid of dinosaurs."

"Why not?"

"They're all dead."

"No they're not."

"Yes, I'm fairly certain they are."

"No they're not. I have one in my bathtub."

"Oh, I see. Well then, I suppose that one I would be afraid of."

"Uncle Jeremy?"

"Yes."

"What else are you afraid of?"

Jeremy closed his eyes, trying to break down the number of questions he would have to answer per hour based on the experience he was currently having.

"My greatest fear is that after cooking a small boy, he would not be completely dead and that he would squeal as I bit into his leg."

Silence filed the car as the nephew digested this. Quizzically, he looked at Jeremy, and Jeremy stared back expressionless with a slow nod, as if agreeing that yes, this actually could happen.

Trudy was silent, knowing her brother's intentions were never to scare but to intimidate. Besides, it gave him some good experience with the stranger side of people. So as he looked from Jeremy to his mom, she could only stare back, eyes wide in mock fear.

The car was silent again as they finally passed through the narrow exit of the parking lot and out onto a wide boulevard with thinly scattered traffic.

Like a speedboat slipping the confines of its harbor, Trudy's husband Jeff gunned the engine and pushed the sedan up the rise ahead that led to the suburbs beyond. As they reached a pleasant cruising speed, the interior was once again alive with inquisition.

"Uncle Jeremy, are you afraid of spiders also?"

Their home was in a sprawling suburb, with houses of the same design and material, yet with boldly different colors. The street was such that it twisted and turned so frequently, with no obvious landmark to guide them, Jeremy was certain that they would eventually end up where they started.

When it seemed that they were hopelessly lost and would never find the end to the maze, a garage door some thirty yards ahead of them began to rise. Like a shuttle approaching the mother ship, the car reached the end of the driveway just as the garage door reached its ascent. Once inside, the car slowed to a perfect stop, whence the garage door began its descent to seal the house again.

Trudy's husband opened the trunk and grabbed the suitcase, heading for the interior door. Jeremy stood there awkwardly, looking for some guidance, until Trudy reached the threshold, turned and motioned for her son to enter, and then waved Jeremy over with a smile.

"Not much has changed since you were here last," she began as they passed through a narrow hallway leading to a laundry room and then entered the kitchen. It was beautifully decorated with solid countertops of stone, cherry cabinets, and hardware that looked hand-molded. From the kitchen, he could see the formal dining room, followed by the spacious living room with notable antiques and furniture. The colors were what Jeremy called suburban light—light beige, a light yellow, with a light brown and white. Yet, Trudy's ability to combine furniture with tapestry colors gave the room its genuine feel of style and comfort. She had the gift of their father, that ability to see pieces and visualize what they could become together.

"Looks great to me," Jeremy complimented as he slid off his coat, shoved his gloves into the pocket, and the scarf into the sleeve. By the door was a long row of coat hooks, and after placing the coat on the nearest open one, he slid his earmuffs over it to keep it in place.

"You definitely have the gift for design," he said as he glanced at his reflection in the black face of the microwave oven. Pushing back the hair along the side of his head, he tugged down his sweater so that it fit tighter, pushed his hands into his pockets, and sauntered toward the living room.

As he entered, he felt the overwhelming presence of their mother, Sarah. Looking at the fireplace and the enormous painting of her above it, graced by two narrow, solemn candles, it reflected a warm and nurturing atmosphere just by the subtle, knowing expression on her face. The painting had been done by their father, one of the largest in his body of work, and without a doubt the favorite of all of them.

At the time it was painted, his adoration for her was at its peak. They had been married for some time, after the three of them had been born in rapid succession, each barely a year apart. She was beautiful, standing in a long, flowing sundress with a vase of daisies, her favorite flower, on the table next to her. Her right hand was on it, dutifully placed, and her left hand was by her side, the palm cupped and facing out, a tribute to her giving nature.

Their father had drawn her hundreds of times in pencil, charcoal, even water color. But this was the only oil he ever did of her. Jeremy studied it casually. He had stared at it hundreds of times, and although she had passed in her early sixties, only a few years ago, it was this version of a young woman in her mid-twenties, just beginning motherhood with her shoulders set back in strength and a confident set of the jaw, he always wanted to remember. Yet, there were times when it seemed there was sadness in her eyes. It was slight, and Jeremy thought he could see it at the corner of her right eye—a slight tear. The harder he seemed to stare at it, the less distinguishable it became.

Turning to gaze at the rest of the room, he noticed the paintings on the walls, all of them by their father. Trudy seemed to have more of an interest in preserving their father's work. Perhaps she had more of a connection to him. As far as he was concerned, he was a man who traveled in the shadows—a father in name only, missing at critical junctions in his life.

He continued gazing at the paintings, barely noticing Trudy walking into the room.

"Would you like one?" she asked.

Jeremy chortled. "He wanted nothing from me, and I want nothing from him."

"The value has been increasing steadily over the past year since he died."

"Is that why you keep them? For the money?"

"No." She hesitated. "I keep them because my dad was a painter. He made a notable living doing it and achieved some regional fame, and they are things I will always have. Heirlooms."

It was a standoff they always had—a revisionist's view of a man's life versus the perspective of someone who couldn't separate the artist from the man. They were both undeterred in their views, knowing the other wouldn't change, yet declarations of opinion were always a reinforcement of these feelings.

"Would you like some wine?" Trudy offered before the silence became awkward.

"Red?" he asked.

"Always," she said and then turned back toward the kitchen. Jeremy followed her.

"Where's Austin?" he asked, shoving his hands into the pocket of his trousers.

"He'll be here soon. He went out to dinner with some of his old high school buddies. Their twentieth reunion is this year, and he's helping to organize it."

From under the counter, she pulled a bottle of merlot, and with the other hand she pulled out a utility drawer and retrieved a waiter's corkscrew. She zipped the foil off the cork effortlessly but began to fumble with the corkscrew.

"Let me help," Jeremy said and gently took the instrument away from her. "Your son's getting big." He spun the corkscrew around, locked the hook onto the lip of the bottle, and sprang the cork free with a pop.

"You haven't seen him in six months, so sure he has definitely grown a few inches." She turned and reached into the cabinet behind her, pulling out four long-stem red wine glasses.

"Perhaps your husband will get the basketball player he's always wanted."

"Don't count on in it. I think the short genes on our side will keep him lower to the ground."

As she was working to arrange the glasses, Jeremy noticed her profile. It was becoming more distinct. Her high cheek bones were becoming more prominent and the nose narrower. She was beginning to resemble their father more and more. When he first noticed it, it intimidated him, but her mannerisms were all his mom's, and the compromise was an easy one to live with.

After filling up the glasses, he set the empty bottle on the counter.

"Don't worry about it," she said, anticipating his question. "There is plenty more downstairs. We hosted a party for a new artist we're showing, and we always overstretch."

"How's the art business?" he asked.

"Not bad. The new pieces are hard to sell lately, but the classics always move easily."

"Like Dad's stuff."

She took a long sip of wine before answering.

"He's not there yet," she answered after a bit of contemplation. "But he's getting closer."

"Does the fact that he shot himself make the paintings more attractive?" The comment was bold and sharply honest, designed to expose an emotional nerve. But Trudy was accustomed to Jeremy's acerbic personality, and she had learned to comment only on the facts, not the intention.

"A good back story always adds to the value of a piece. How's the real estate business?"

"Tight, but I'm making it."

"Any permanent woman in the making?" she asked playfully.

"There's a few options," he shyly revealed, "but none worth having."

"You're in your late thirties. You'd better be thinking about finding someone, or you may never find one at all."

"There's always someone. Trust me, there is plenty of depth at that position. How about Austin?"

At that moment, the front door opened, and a baritone voice boomed across the rom.

"Honey, I'm home!"

"Ask him yourself," she replied. "Go see your brother. I'm going to check on my husband and see if he actually got our son in the bathtub."

Bombastic in his approach, the youngest of the three contained all of the joy of having survived a near-death experience. In contrast to Jeremy, Austin was a believer that today is the last day and needs to be lived as such. He was warm and embracing, a true lover of the company of people, and his plumpness contrasted with the leanness of Jeremy and Trudy. He was a connoisseur of the finer things in life with regards to dining and celebrations. Dressed in a thick, black, long wool coat, he accented his overcoat with a brilliant scarf and a matching short cap revealing brilliantly red ears.

"Bro!" he bellowed as he strode through the living room and approached the kitchen with arms open.

Jeremy barely had time to put down his glass before a thick set of arms crossed over his chest and almost pushed the air out of his lungs.

"Hi, Austin," Jeremy replied weakly.

"Jeremy! How's you doin'?"

"Just fine," he said.

"How's life in the Sunshine State?"

"Actually, that's Florida. I live on the coast of Georgia."

"Whatever! It's sunny there too—right?"

Jeremy just nodded.

Grabbing a glass of wine, Austin took a huge gulp and hesitated as it flushed its way down his throat.

"Where's my sister?" he yelled.

Trudy came around the corner, only to be immediately bear-hugged by her younger brother.

"Ick," she responded as he splashed a wet kiss on her cheek.

"What'd I miss?" he said, leaving her disheveled and standing slightly askew. "I know what I missed. Bourbon! Got any? Wine's nice, but I like a horse with some kick."

"Yes, I do, but nothing right now until we talk. Besides, should you let your dinner settle? You obviously drank it."

"Make it quick," he said and then took another gulp of wine, nearly finishing the glass. He leaned against the counter impatiently, his girth positioned uneasily against the low ledge.

"Todd just got into the bathtub, and he'll be there for a while, so we'll have time to talk." She went into the dining room and opened the center drawer of the china cabinet. Pulling out a well-traveled white envelope, she set it on the sink island in the center of the kitchen as the two men crowded around.

"I received this in the mail the other day. Sliding her hand into the ragged, open end, she produced a business envelope. It had already been unsealed, and Trudy had scanned the contents without really studying it. "Apparently, some letters were lost at the post office, and they are being delivered now." She hesitated as she scanned the letter once again. "And this is one that was sent to me."

"So," Austin said, his mouth longing for the taste of the liquor he knew was in the next room.

"It's from Aunt Gracie. This letter was sent a few months before she died of the heart attack."

"Which was about four months after Dad died," Jeremy added.

Trudy nodded, ripped open the envelope, and began to read:

Dearest Trudy,

I know that losing your father is difficult, probably more so than losing your mother, as you were especially close to him. I just want you to know that I am here for you. The horrible and sudden way in which he passed has shocked all of us, and we are stunned that he did it so suddenly without reaching out to any of us.

At my age, I've lost my share of family and friends, and I may not be long for this world myself, but from it I've learned about grief. It can be deep and seem endless. Please be careful not to let it smother you. If you do, it will affect everything you do and what you hope to become.

I know that it had an effect on your father. When he lost Deborah, he truly lost a piece of himself, and he never was the same. When he lost Sara, something burned out in him and was never lit again. I remember my brother as a young man, vibrant, gregarious, and inquisitive. Grief took that all away.

"Who's Deborah?" Austin interrupted. Trudy held up her finger in a request for patience and continued to read.

The main reason I am writing is that your father needed to trust someone with something of extreme value to him. Attached to this letter is a key, and that key opens a storage locker at the Shurlock Home storage facility on the north side of town. Being that I live in Arizona and do not plan to visit the Midwest anytime soon, I felt you should have it as soon as possible. I do not know what is in there, but I hope that it is beneficial to all of you. Take care, and I love you all.

Sincerely,
Aunt Gracie

Finishing, she set the letter down on the counter and then produced a small key that was taped to the bottom of the letter.

She handed it to Jeremy, who examined it, flipping it in his palm. "Just a small key to a padlock," he deduced.

"So who's Deborah?" Austin asked again.

Trudy looked at Jeremy, who returned her gaze. Under his inquisitive stare, she could only shrug.

"There's nothing in his paintings related to a Deborah. There are a lot of portraits, but they were all commissions, and nothing relates to that name."

"Could she have been a girlfriend?" Austin postulated.

"I doubt it," Jeremy replied. "He may have ignored us, but I know he loved Mom. They were inseparable."

"If there was a girlfriend, I'm sure she would have shown up somewhere, either in a piece he created or in letters or some sort of correspondence."

"Perhaps that is what the key will lead us to," Jeremy stated as he set it down on top of the letter laid out before them.

The following morning, the sun rose on a frigid sky. Cloudless, it was bright and blinding against the snowy landscape. Its apparent warmth from the window masked the subzero wind that cut sharply around corners and knifed through the thickest garments. Jeremy was drinking a fresh cup of coffee and looking through the patio window facing the neighbor's backyard. The children were struggling to play in the subzero cline, so heavily wrapped that they appeared as small bubble people in a moon-like environment. In the bushes near the window, he saw small balls of feathers deep inside the shrubs, sparrows choosing to remain in as guarded a location as possible rather than look for food. Normally they would have seen him and darted away in a cloud of brown streaks, but today they existed only as small tufts of feathers and darting black eyes, staring at him as if pleading him not to come toward them and make them move.

Having given all of his winter clothes away, he now substituted layered flannel and cotton for a borrowed, knitted brown sweater with yellow deer playing and small pine trees in the background. Once they were ready to leave, he would throw on a sweatshirt, and he was ready.

His nephew was already awake, and after spending an awkward half an hour with Jeremy, the young boy was completely bored with his uncle and easily enthralled when asked to go ice skating with his father and few of his school friends. When he was gone, the three of them would depart.

Hearing a stumbling from the direction of the living room, Austin appeared. Somewhat disheveled and with a distinct redness in his eyes, he awkwardly found his way to the kitchen, reached for a coffee cup from the cabinets, and with the utmost concentration, poured some coffee.

"How did you sleep?" Jeremy asked.

Austin lifted the cup with both hands and slowly took a sip. Taking as much as he could, he then held the cup tightly and shrugged a reply.

Jeremy waited until Austin had had a few more sips before making another inquiry.

"So what do you think we will find today?"

"Could be anything," Austin replied as the caffeine began to subdue the lasting effects of the bourbon. "My guess is probably the same as yours—paintings. I mean, that's all Dad ever did."

"That's what I was thinking too. I mean it's not like he spent any time with us."

Austin smirked. "You need to get past this, Jeremy."

"Get past what?"

"This neglect thing you keep bringing up."

Jeremy paused for a second. "I don't think it's neglect."

"Sure you do. It's just deep inside, and it manifests itself as anger. In fact, I think you're bitter about it."

"No, not bitter."

"Trust me; you sound bitter."

"Doesn't it bother you that he was never there while we were kids? Always gone somewhere for a commission, always missing for weeks to paint landscape, never really around for anything we did?"

Austin thought for a second. "It did, but it doesn't anymore. He was Dad whether he was here or not, and I know he loved us. It was just hard for him to get close to us. For some reason, there was something about being near us that he couldn't cope with. Distance worked for him." Looking into his cup, he realized it was almost empty and turned to walk back to the coffee pot.

"What do you think Trudy would—"

Austin held up his hand while turning toward the coffee pot. "Don't go there. You want to know what Trudy thinks, ask Trudy." Austin filled his cup again and then casually scanned the kitchen.

"Have you seen any Danish? They usually have Danish."

"They're on the dining room table. You passed them on the way in here."

"Oh," Austin said, somewhat taken aback by his morning blindness. "How could I have missed those?" He swaggered over to the assortment and scanned them for his first victim, dangling his fingers over them as if playing a keyboard.

A loud crash of traffic tumbled down the stairs as father and son shuttled quickly through the kitchen, the youngest with his blades over his shoulders and the newest cold weather gear tightly bounding him in. They passed through so quickly Jeremy could only nod and raise his cup to acknowledge the young boy's toothless smile and weak wave. Trudy was following close behind but stopped at the edge of the kitchen. She already had her coat on and smiled proudly as she watched her son enter the garage.

With the sound of an engine, and the rumble of the garage door, they were off, leaving the three of them to coordinate and begin their quest. As Trudy stood at the edge of the dining room, she pulled out her smart phone and slid through the screens, intent on searching for a specific fact. Once it revealed itself, she stood straight and took charge of the trio.

"The storage facility is by the airport, not too far and fairly easy to find. We should be there in twenty minutes." She proceeded toward the garage with a key in one hand and her phone in the other, Jeremy and Austin following quietly. For the second time, an engine revved, a garage door rumbled, and a vehicle departed.

The SUV was quiet until Trudy eased the vehicle off the ramp and into the mainstream of the interstate. Traffic was light with it being a weekend, so it was an easy adjustment into cruise mode. Austin broke the silence as he dusted the sugar flakes off his colored deer sweater.

"So what do you think we'll find there?" he asked.

The silence was telling as the two siblings thought about an answer.

"Hope it wasn't an ice sculpture," he answered to himself and chuckled.

"I know what Trudy hopes," Jeremy suddenly blurted out. "She's thinking along the lines of Wyeth's *Helga* collection, a collection now worth tens of millions of dollars."

"Don't be silly," Trudy answered, although the uncomfortable silence afterwards made it apparent that it was exactly what she was thinking. "What about you, Jeremy? What are you thinking? Stocks, bonds, securities, deeds?"

"Perhaps. And you, Austin?" Jeremy volleyed back. "Hoping for a forgotten whiskey archive?"

Austin formed a fist and began rubbing his knuckles against the steam forming on the window. "Cheese," he replied, "lots and lots of cheese."

With this verbal display of idiocy, they were all silent again until the SUV slid over to the off ramp leading to the airport and slowly descended to a stoplight.

The business park where the storage facility was located was large in expanse but little in stature. Following the digital directions, she was guided to its entrance where it stood out from the other facilities because of its high iron fencing, mechanical gate lifts, and guard shack at the entrance. Following the directions, Trudy honked twice and then waited patiently as the first set of gates slowly opened. She approached one of the parking spaces, choosing one at the end nearest the door to the guard shack and the second set of gates, which appeared to open into the compound.

The three of them exited the car and walked through the steel door into the office. In front of them was a high counter that stretched the length of room and was about chest high. Startled, the be-speckled, roughly shorn, young man suddenly popped his head up. Like in a school photograph, Timothy Akers was now present and accounted for.

"Can I help you?" he said in an uncertain voice, eyeing each of them in turn, like a Western bartender measuring up the three strangers in town.

"We have a key to this storage facility," Trudy offered as she laid the key and a notecard with the storage bin number on it. Akers gazed at the key and then the card and then back to the key again.

As this inspection was occurring, Austin wandered over to a wall displaying a variety of tapes, signs, and locks of variable sizes.

"Do you sell much of this stuff?" Austin asked.

Tim paused from his inspection. "Not really." He adjusted his glasses and walked over to his computer screen. "Most people want garbage bags. They try to fill up their bin with stuff, and when there's no more room, they finally decide to toss stuff instead of paying for a bigger bin."

"What happens if they don't pay?"

Tim took a sheet of paper with a map on it. "We give them thirty days, and then we auction off what's inside."

"Anything good?"

"Not really. Mostly clothes and toys. Last month though, some lady's trust fund ran out, and we had to open it using the universal key over there." He nodded to a pair of well-worn blue bolt cutters. "Turns out she had stuffed all of the dogs she had ever owned. There must have been a dozen dogs in there, some of them so old they were falling apart."

"What'd you do with them?"

"Just threw them into the dumpster, but the weird thing is, by the next morning, half of them were gone."

"Maybe they weren't all that dead." Austin chuckled.

Tim thought for a second. "No, they were dead all right." He then presented the map in front of Trudy and marked one of the dozens of squares with a red highlighter.

"The bin is located here in the tower, third floor." Tim adjusted his glasses. "Will you be closing out the account?"

"No, probably not. Can I let you know when we leave?"

"Sure. Then we'll forward the balance to you?"

"Me?"

"Uhh . . . yeah. I mean, I assume you're this phone number. It's listed on the account. When the balance runs low, we're supposed to call it, and a deposit is made."

"What's the number?'

Tim checked the screen again, wrote the number down on the map, and showed Trudy.

"That's my great-aunt's number. She's deceased."

"Oh, sorry. Oh then, you need a copy of . . ."

"You know, how about we deal with this when we leave."

"Oh, fine, um . . . whatever you want to do."

"That's what I want to do."

"Okay, just drive to the gate. I can see you from here, and I'll let you in."

Trudy smiled politely, turned, and led the troupe out of the office.

Getting back into the car, she drove to the gate, and true to his word, it rolled away, allowing them to pass through.

"Here, Jeremy, you're the keeper of the key." She tossed it into his lap.

"Okay" was his only reply.

"You've been especially quiet," Trudy said.

"Not much to say."

"Scared about what we'll find?"

"No, just apprehensive." Finding the tower was easy, and she parked right by to the security door. "I mean what if it really is cheese." He smiled as he left the car.

Walking through the heavy steel purple door, they entered the large concrete-walled catacombs. The sounds of their feet echoed in the empty hallways, the white concrete walls broken up only by the even spacing of the purple and lavender doors. At the end of the hallway was an open elevator, painted in the company's colors, and as directed, they walked toward it.

Encased in plated steel, the elevator was as strong and secure as the rest of the complex. Trudy pushed the button for the third floor. Obediently, the doors slid close, and the motor hummed as they were lifted to the desired floor. The silence between them seemed awkward, and Jeremy shifted his weight as if to say something. Austin and Trudy looked at him quizzically, but he just smiled and crossed his arms.

Reaching the third floor, Trudy checked the letter once more to ensure they were at the right level. When the doors opened, the hallway appeared eerily similar to the one they left, except there was no outside door at the end. Trudy left the elevator, with her brothers close behind, counted three doors on her right, stopped, turned, and stared at a purple door identical to the dozen or so that they had passed.

"Here," she said. "This one." She nodded at a door with the number 314 above it in a heavy yellow stencil.

They stood in front of it in a half circle, Jeremy in the center, each hesitant about initiating the action. For Trudy and Austin, it was easy; Jeremy had the key, so Jeremy should open the door. For Jeremy, there was this sudden guilt that he was about to look at something that was meant to be private and never discovered. Yet, here he was with the key, the location, and the permission.

Stepping up quietly, he pulled the padlock away from the door, turning it upside down to expose the open hole. Sliding the key in easily, he gave it a quick turn. Obediently it snapped open. He slid the lock off and handed it to Austin while he flipped back the latch and bent over to pull the handle on the louvered door. In a quick rush of purple and dust, the door receded into the ceiling.

The room was dark, with only shadows along the sides and what appeared to be a large bale in the center. Squinting, Jeremy took a step forward, allowing the motion-detecting sensor to engage the lights and illuminate the entire room. A box of secrets hidden for many years was now suddenly on display, beckoning for its moment.

The room was small, twenty feet by ten feet, yet the objects in the room seemed to be evenly spaced with what appeared to be frames along the walls.

Everything was covered and arranged, leaving plenty of space in between to walk around.

Somewhat dumbfounded, they slowly toured the room with Trudy being the first to actually move the covers. Approaching the set nearest the door, she cautiously pulled away the mover's blanket, exposing four empty frames, each constructed of a different wood.

"Storage," she replied. "Just storage."

"Another room of junk," Austin exclaimed, exhaling heavily with disappointment.

"But there must be something," Jeremy said, pulling the blanket off the centerpiece in the room, revealing an old steamer trunk, latched but not locked, its thick tongue of a clasp hanging down in front.

Trudy continued to expose additional empty frames until she got to the fifth stack. After pulling the cover away in a dusty cloud, a wonderful oil painting of their mother was exposed. She was very young and beamed brightly with the small bundle of a child on her lap. The girl in the painting held a silent smile, with yellow bows knitted into subtle red hair, her right hand clasping their mother's blouse.

The brothers turned away from the trunk and studied the painting before them.

"Is that you?" Austin asked.

Trudy shook her head slowly. "I've always been a brunette, unless Dad wanted to paint me as a redhead."

"That must be you," Jeremy stated. "It looks just like you. I can even see the resemblance to Mom."

"Remember, guys—it's a painting, not a photograph. It can be anything Dad wanted it to be."

Trudy continued to uncover more paintings but still looked back at the first one she found. As she exposed the others, she found one of Jeremy wearing a small gray sweater with a ball, and a painting of one-year-old Austin in a cowboy suit and a rocking horse, a picture window facing a pasture in the background. And the last picture on the wall had a small child with a pinwheel in one hand and a crayon in the other. The look of whimsy in her eyes was captured perfectly.

"This is me," Trudy blurted out, yet still unsure as she looked at both, trying to contrast and compare. It fell on deaf ears, however, as the brothers had set upon the steamer trunk. It opened easily and revealed a treasure filled to the top. Photographs—hundreds, if not thousands of them. Some just quick Polaroids, others sitting portraits. And all of them, every single one that Jeremy and Austin pulled out by the handful, were of them as children. There were class photographs, pictures at the zoo, the circus, on picnics, in their backyard, at the dinner table, everywhere in the house where they grew up. Most of the pictures were of them as young kids, but there were some of them in school and on the playground.

There were dozens of Trudy and Jeremy and Austin, and also of the little girl in the painting, many of them with the kids interacting together. At birthday parties, in a sandbox, swimming in a shallow children's pool, everywhere it seemed.

"Do you think she was a distant cousin or something?" Austin asked as he sorted through a handful like playing cards.

Jeremy shrugged. "I don't remember any mention of her. Mom was always good at keeping in touch with the family."

Intrigued, Trudy came over to the chest and scanned through the collection before them. With her keen eye for detail, she reached down and with two nimble fingers pulled at the worn, crumpled edge of a manila envelope. It slid out easily from the pile, revealing a surprisingly large envelope full of papers. As the brothers continued excavating through the stacks of photos, Trudy reached into the envelope and pulled out two legal documents. Wandering off to the side, she placed her fingers to her forehead in concentration as she digested the contents.

"I don't get it," Austin finally exclaimed. "Here's a guy who didn't care whether we lived or died, didn't involve himself at all in our lives on any level, and there are these piles of pictures of us that he kept. What the hell happencd?"

"Deborah happened," Trudy suddenly blurted out, examining the birth certificate and then switching to the death certificate. "Then viral pneumonia happened. She wasn't even a year old."

Suddenly, as if a whisper had echoed in each of their ears, they turned to face a large frame, four feet wide and equally as tall and covered over with a thick, light blue comforter. Jeremy reached over and pulled away the cover, revealing a giant photograph of a wonderfully happy family with four young children. Their father had done a wonderful portrait of himself, smiling, lean, athletic, with thin, feathery sideburns, a strong shock of black hair, and ruddy cheeks bookending a toothy grin. His eyes showed a pride they rarely saw, almost enlightenment at being with his equally delighted wife and four small children.

"And she was our little sister," Jeremy added. They all stared at the small cherub with red hair positioned between the two young, gleaming boys and adorable little girl with brown curls.

Arthur's Letter

———•———

"So THERE REALLY ISN'T ANY hope," Arthur said, facing his son, Steve, both of them seated in the purple and pink plastic chairs lined neatly throughout the health center's waiting room.

"No, Dad, there isn't," his son said. His arms were folded, forming a bridge between the arms of the chair, fingers laced tightly in the center. His head hung down, staring at the grey and red speckled carpet, eyes beginning to well with tears. Before they could begin to pool and fall to the ground, he looked up at the slumping shape of his father in the chair in front of him.

Suddenly, he saw him as if it were the first time. Gone was the strong man he knew as a child. The man with shoulders as thick as a beam, who would play catch with him until dark, and then only stopping until the ball had rolled into the blackness of some shrubs, or under a car, left until the morning when the light was better. A man who, when he got home in the evenings, would eat a quick meal and then physically ambush him as he went to finish his homework or lie down to relax by the TV. With all the hard work he did, and as tired as he was, his dad always found the energy to challenge him, to try to beat him, proving to Steve he was still in charge.

Steven remembered those days as a teenager well. The roughness of his father's hands from handling the mortar and the fired clay bricks, and the power they had as he would clamp down on Arthur's wrist or ankle viselike, in a grip as aggressive as it was reassuring—that he would always be there to catch him. As he grew older, he became nimble enough to avoid the sharp grasps and suffocating hugs that always ended the matches in his father's favor. But Steven could never keep it up long enough and eventually succumbed due to a slow stop or an anticipated dodge that his father was able to take advantage of.

The man was unbeatable—eternal.

The same man was now before him, at seventy-two, a shadow of the workhorse he once was. The clothes he wore now fit him so loosely from the sudden weight loss, they appeared to be hung on him more than they were being worn. The pants were deeply wrinkled, seams lost as the fabric bunched together when he sat down. His shoes were scuffed on the outside instead of the toe because they would rub together when he shuffled, the cuffs worn and frayed from being dragged along the floor. Thick black glasses covered a face blotched brown and white and wrinkled from summers in the sun. He was a man in twilight.

And behind those lenses were the memories of a life together. A father and son, one building the life of the other, the other adding richness and purpose to a life of living.

"You told me once that you weren't a contractor," Steven began, "that contractors were the guys in the buildings doing contracts. That you were a brick layer. Because that's what you did, that's what you were. You always seemed to understand the truth in everything and the reality of what things were. Do you understand what is going to happen?"

The old man contemplated what Steve had said and shifted in his seat. On the back of his left hand was a small, square, clean bandage. It contrasted sharply with his dark skin, browned and freckled from exposure. Hard calluses stood out on his thick fingers, the price for placing hundreds of thousands of bricks neatly on the mortar and in a level line. Reaching over to the bandage, he pushed it down firmly and held it in place, despite the adhesive that was holding it to the skin, as if wishing it would absorb and purge the demons under his skin.

"That is what I was," he replied with some confidence, but after he said it, his eyes drifted away and looked casually out the window into the parking lot. "And this," he tapped the bandage softly, "is what it is."

Struggling to push himself up, his son jumped to his aid and helped him to his feet. Reaching a solid stance, he reached out for his son's hand. "Let's go home," he whispered.

Opening the thick, wooden front door, they entered the small three-bedroom house that Arthur had paid off decades before and where he had raised his two boys and lived with his wife for forty-three years until her passing two years before. They were instantly greeted by his six-year-old granddaughter, Celia, her cherubic face dominated by a broad smile. She bouncing over to them from the kitchen at the end of the hall, her long, brown hair waving around her head like wild grass in the wind, waving, her eyes alit with curiosity.

"Grandpa, this came for you!" she squealed. Beaming with pride, she presented it to him with such nobility as if she were Mercury himself.

"What could this be?" he chimed in a playful singsong. "Is it Christmas?"

She shook her head.

"Is it Easter?"

She shook her head again.

"Perhaps it is my birthday." He chortled.

Not sure how to answer, she pulled back the thin hair that had fallen across her face and gazed at him with distant blue eyes yearning for a direction.

He leaned down, close to her ear, and whispered, "It's not my birthday."

She giggled, grabbed his arm, and led him toward the living room.

As he was being guided, he realized that his son was no longer near him and had progressed down the hallway and into the kitchen at its end. He saw his firstborn bent over the shoulder of his wife, her eyes closed tightly with concern, his back shuddering from the sobs as he told her the results of his father's tests.

"Come on, Grandpa!" she pleaded, as she now had both hands on his forearm, pulling with all her might to get him to the sofa where, once seated, he would be at her mercy. Playing into the game after withdrawing from the scene in the kitchen, he pretended to pull away, faking a determined effort to resist while pleading for his life. As she giggled from all of the over-dramatization, the envelope in her hand fell away and landed at his feet, face up. For a second, there was a pause in the drama, as Arthur scrutinized the address and the sender on the yellowing business letter.

Sensing the sudden seriousness, she stopped laughing and grew quiet.

"What is it, Grandpa?" she asked softly. Focusing on the letter before him, lying directly between his legs like a sacrifice, he softly laid his hand on his granddaughter's head.

"Pick this up for me, will you, dear?"

Obediently, she complied, still sad about the sudden end of the playing. Bending sharply, she picked it up and tentatively handed it to her grandfather.

With a withering hand, he took the envelope, tore the end off, and then reached in with two fingers to pull out a folded, blank sheet of paper that enclosed a check written out for $10,000. He recognized the name as a developer he had worked with in the past.

Checking the date, written in the same month ten years before, he chuckled and slipped the check back into the envelope, folded it in half, and pushed it into the breast pocket of his shirt.

With a solemn stare, he put his hands into his pockets and glared at the innocent face of his granddaughter.

"The letter is from the zoo, and it says they have room for one more monkey."

His granddaughter immediately caught the humor and grinned, eagerly waiting for the punch line, her hands curled into fists tucked neatly under her smile. "That means you!" he bellowed as she squealed and darted into the kitchen for help.

After dinner, Arthur settled into what was once considered his smoking chair. With his son's family gathering their things as they were preparing to leave, he reached over to the phone on the end table next to him. He glanced briefly at the buttons and then decided it was time to call. After they had left, he lifted the receiver and dialed the number he knew by heart. It rang three times and then was picked up. The deep hello seemed to carry through the phone and into the room itself.

"Reverend Tibbits?" Arthur inquired.

"Speaking."

"It's Arthur Chandler." He paused. "I received a bit of bad news today, and I was wondering if I could meet you tomorrow."

"Certainly, Arthur." His tone expressed regret about the cancer he knew Arthur was fighting.

"Could we meet at Veteran's Park, say about 10:00?"

"I will be there, Arthur. See you then."

Hearing it click off, he replaced the receiver back into the cradle. Arthur once again pressed against the bandage on his hand. He could have taken it off hours ago, but he was afraid to look at the ugly face of the beast within him. It was already making its appearance on the instruments he used to measure his vitality. Thinking about his meeting tomorrow, he thought over the things he had done in the span of his life. Mostly good—but some bad. Some very bad. This would be difficult, he knew, but a sign of contrition had appeared, and he needed to atone.

The park where they were to meet wasn't very far from where he lived. Normally he would walk the distance, but rising this morning had been a little taxing, and it was getting difficult to reach that energy level. The poison in his veins was slowly eroding his strength, and on some days when he was prepared to fight, the battle was joined. Today, however, was not one of those days. Despite the fact that the sun, which he always relied on as reinforcement, was brilliant, the sky empty of clouds, an icy blue pallet stretching out above him, the effort wasn't there.

He dressed according to the coolness of the early autumn morning and then called a cab for the short ride there. With little volume on a Saturday morning, it didn't take long for a red Caprice to pull in front of the house and honk twice. Negotiating the front stairs with a cane and two bad feet, he made it down the brick path and to the rear door of the car breathing heavily. "Veteran's Park," he said in a shallow voice. With a nod, the driver pulled away.

Reaching the edge of the block-long park, he could see that the expanses of open grass were dotted with the colors of children's uniforms playing for a multitude of teams. Their squeals and shouts could be heard through the door's glass, yet he scanned it all, focusing on a small monument in the far corner of the park.

Tapping the driver on the shoulder, he told him to head for the monument. Nodding again, the driver drove to the end of the block and then turned right to where there was an obelisk positioned in the center of a wide expanse of neatly arranged pavers. He paid the driver ten dollars for a four-dollar fare. While he was struggling to get out of the backseat, the driver watched his fare carefully in the rearview mirror. Seeing him swing his feet out and hesitate, the driver asked if he needed any help. With a sharp wave, Arthur ignored the request. After some effort, he was able to push himself up and out of the car, shutting the door firmly.

For a moment, he stood there and gazed at the gracefully ascending stone monument, its four blond limestone sides perfectly angled and sanded to reach a shallow triangle eighteen feet above the ground. Each side was engraved with a conflict title. Three sides were engraved with their own chapter. World War II, World War I, and the Civil War were deeply etched in the stone at the top, and below each title were long lists of full names and the conflicts in which they perished. Anthony Cerbic—Cold Harbor. William Taylor Mays—Chateau Thierry. Richard Farmer—Anzio. Ernst Chalmer—Tarawa.

On the fourth side was a shorter list, each describing the conflicts in which the shorter list of names fell. It started with Korea at the top and ended with Afghanistan on the bottom, leaving plenty of room toward the bottom of the monument to list additional sacrifices.

Around the obelisk were brick pavers, alternating in blue and red, creating an ever widening circle around the monument, the last ending forty-five feet away from the center of the obelisk. Positioned at mid-points in an inner circle halfway between the inner and outer ring were eight benches, each topped with a matching limestone slab four feet wide and eight feet long, perfectly positioned on a pedestal of solid limestone blocks. Two benches faced each side, giving the visitor a place to sit and reflect. There were no playing fields in this area, just trees and native plants that added a feeling of calmness and serenity. He loved this place. It was his favorite place. It was the place that he had built using all the skills he knew in chiseling and masonry. This was his park, and it would be five years old this year.

Finding a bench that was partially shaded, he sat down awkwardly and posted his cane between his legs like a standard. He stared at the face of the obelisk in front of him, the Civil War tablet, and slowly read the names. They were mostly Irish, that being the first nationality to settle in the area, but he could identify a little Swedish and German too. He liked sitting here because it reflected the true heritage of the old town. Not the Hispanic names that were beginning to appear on the opposite side, the side with the most recent conflicts. Those were the ones who were invading the town, trying to change it to their ways, bringing their culture here along with the poverty and lower values. And why were they here? To run away from something, not toward a better society as these forefathers were trying to establish. He shook his head lightly at the quiet realization that soon none of this would matter. He wouldn't be sticking around to see how it ended.

"Arthur?" a strong voice from beside him asked.

Arthur turned to see a large, burly man with a rounded face and a clean-shaven head.

"Reverend," Arthur said in reply, taken aback somewhat by the startled look on the man's face. It then occurred to him that although they had talked many times over the phone in the past, they hadn't met for some months—thirty pounds and four chemotherapy treatments ago. He realized he probably looked slightly different. Perhaps gaunt.

"Sorry, Reverend, I'm not in the best shape I've ever been. I've lost a little weight."

Realizing his expression was inadvertently honest, the reverend quickly shifted to a passive demeanor and compassionate smile.

"So, Arthur," he began in a soft voice as he sat down next to him on the bench, "how are you feeling?"

"Right now, okay. Maybe a little stiff, some soreness." He paused. "But very soon, it will be over."

"I see. How can I help you?"

"Well, I guess I just need to get something off my chest. Something that happened a long time ago, that has been plaguing me." He began to twirl his cane as he contemplated what he was about to say.

"Reverend . . . do you believe in ghosts?" he began.

"I believe in the Holy Spirit and in the angels."

"You know, Reverend," he waved his hand in front of him as if clearing away smoke, "that's the company line. My question is . . . do you believe in ghosts?"

"No, I don't."

"I didn't either . . . until recently."

"Are you fearful of becoming one?"

"No . . . not becoming one. I've been seeing them in my dreams." Arthur looked away in the distance, as if searching to see if they were hiding in the landscape, listening.

"Do they talk to you? Do they say anything?"

Arthur shook his head. "They just stare at me. Standing there, as if waiting."

The reverend sat there for a second, crossed his fingers, and laid them patiently in his lap.

"What do you think they want?"

"Me," he said.

"You mean as if they were couriers or guides to the other side?"

Arthur looked down at his feet, and the reverend could now see the fear. It was a fear he had seen many times before at the hospice—the realization that mortality wasn't a concept anymore or even a diagnosis. Now it was a date and a time.

"You see, Reverend, when I first started to lay bricks, I struggled. It was hard to make ends meet, and there were a lot of Mondays where I didn't know if I could make it to a Friday. I worked out of it with time and some luck and occasionally with some favors from some contractors."

Arthur hesitated. He looked up, placed both hands upon his cane, and shifted his weight to be more comfortable on the bench. "There was one contractor I knew . . . well I never met him. Just talked to him on the phone. I did some special favors for him over the years. Real quiet stuff. And when it was done, I'd receive a check in the mail. A big one."

"Did you do a lot of favors for him?"

"Over the years . . . a lot. Enough where I could pay off my house . . . save for the future . . . help my kids if they needed it."

"What kind of favors were they?" the reverend asked hesitantly.

"Packages," he answered.

"Packages?"

"Packages . . . human packages."

The color left the reverend's face. "You mean that you would transport people from place to place?"

Arthur had a stillness about him. By revealing the truth about what he did, he had intended it to be a cleansing. It was something he felt would be difficult, but it was within him like a solid mass, and unlike the tumor rotting away his liver, this tumor he could exorcise. Starting from the beginning, he hoped to extricate all of it.

"When I was working on a building, I would get a phone call from this man, and he would say he had a package for me that I needed to dispose of. So I would go out to the job site at night when no one was around and reveal a section of a wall or clean out some cinderblock to make a small, hollow section. Once I was done, I would go back to my truck and wait. A van would pull up. Two or three men would come out, haul a large plastic package out of the back, place it in the opening I had created, and then leave. Once that was done, I would go back and seal up the wall."

The reverend swallowed hard. "How do you know these packages were people?"

"During one of the times when I was laying brick, I heard a moaning sound coming from the bag. I was scared, so I thought about taking the wall apart and trying to save whoever it was. Then I head the Spanish, *"Aqua, aqua."* It was one of those damn Mexicans. Moving into the town. Living in shacks on the outskirts. Drinking, stealing, trashing the place. Lowering the town. I just finished my wall and went home."

They sat there in silence, Arthur staring at the obelisk, stoic and proud, with the stern, sullen look of a man who was the champion of civility, a man certain of a righteous path, whose journey could only begin with a word from the gentleman next to him. The reverend sat hunched, head bowed, staring at the twitching fingers rapping on his knees. His shoulders were bowed down by the sudden weight, a mass of truth that now seemed on the verge of bending him down to his knees. Over the years, he had heard countless confessions, endless appeals for Christian clemency for infidelities, extortion, vanity, and jealousy. There were thousands of pleas for even the simplest felonies that could even remotely prevent them from passing into God's kingdom.

But none had ever deliberately led to the death of another. This man before him had willingly let another human being suffer and die without even the slightest turn of human kindness. As the preacher was tormenting over the willful loss of a soul, he glimpsed at the confessor seated stoically next to him, arms now crossed, back as straight as the lampposts around them.

"How many times did this happen?" the reverend asked softly.

"Many."

The reverend winced at the thought of a platoon of souls lost about the city. As he mentally added the number of buildings Arthur had built in the town, the possibility became mind-numbing.

"You must confess this," the reverend said suddenly. His head slowly nodded at the justice this would bring. "You must confess this to end this suffering."

Arthur turned and looked him with the hard stare of someone who had spent decades leveling courses of brick with only the steady guide of a retina.

"But I am," he said coolly.

"I can't give that to you," the reverend said quietly, barely audible. His features seemed smaller now, as if falling into his face, disappearing from the sudden pressure. As he was listening, he flipped through the buildings that Arthur had constructed over twenty-five years in this town—the Archer Tool and Die facility, VFW Hall 151, the McDonalds on Route 171, the grocery store off of Sebastian Street, the daycare center by Alabama Court, the new Christian school adjunct to his rectory. All of them tombs.

The pastor took a deep breath. "Arthur, what you've done is wrong. It's murder, a cardinal sin. The only absolution is to confess in this world and face the challenges and penalties that follow."

"But don't you see? I'm out of time. I thought that perhaps you could explain after I'm gone."

"You must confess the sins against man to man and let the cards fall where they may. The forgiveness you are asking for can only be given to you by God. I am just a messenger and a pathway to the Bible. I cannot determine your fate once your time has come."

Arthur sat and thought, and the reverend continued to compose himself after recovering from the shock.

"I understand," Arthur said finally.

"If there is some way you would let me know where these people are, perhaps we can reconcile with their families."

"I wouldn't know where to begin."

The pastor sighed in disbelief. "If you change your mind, please call me. I will help you as much as I can."

Arthur pursed his lips and nodded slowly. Patting him softly on the shoulder, the pastor slowly stood and quietly walked away, his head down, hands clasped tightly behind his back as he took long strides away.

Arthur sat in the park for a while, watching the shadow of the obelisk come closer to his feet like an encroaching tide. Finally he stood, almost stumbling forward from the numbness in his legs from sitting for so long. He walked to the edge of the paver circle unsteadily and then turned slowly and gazed back at the eight rectangular benches and the tall obelisk standing over them.

Speaking strongly but quietly, he gazed over his creation.

"Gentlemen, please forgive me," he said. Then he slowly walked away through the arboreal canopied walks.

About the Author

GREG WRIGHT CURRENTLY LIVES IN River Forest, a western suburb of Chicago, with his wife and ten-year-old son. With a passion for life, a healthy desire to ask "what if," and a graduate-level education, he has enjoyed writing his whole life.